THE PEGASUS
ADVENTURES

THE PEGASUS ADVENTURES

Norman Turner

Book Guild Publishing
Sussex, England

First published in Great Britain in 2007 by
The Book Guild Ltd
Pavilion View
19 New Road
Brighton, BN7 2LU

Typesetting in Baskerville by
Keyboard Services, Luton, Bedfordshire

Printed in Great Britain by
CPI Bath

A catalogue record for this book is available from
The British Library

ISBN 978 1 84624 086 7

To Thomas, Lewis and Benjamin

Contents

BOOK 1

Adventure on the *Pegasus*

Chapter 1

The sun was exceptionally bright as the two teenage boys walked up onto the cliff top overlooking the beautiful sheltered bay spread out before them. The sea was mirroring the sun as its incandescent shimmer made it difficult to stare at without hurting the eyes.

'This must be one of the best days we have had this year,' said Tom Bascombe to his pal James Purdy.

'We've been really lucky to have been given today off work,' James responded.

The two lads were a few months into their fifteenth year, but had already been working for a year as apprentices to a local boat builder. They considered themselves very lucky indeed to have been accepted as apprentices by the boatyard.

The year was 1727, and times were hard in the part of the West Country port where they both lived. Tom's father worked with two colleagues on a rowing boat, which they took out to sea to catch fish and hopefully sell on their return. During very bad weather the trio couldn't attempt setting out to sea. It followed that the Bascombe family income was somewhat spasmodic. Tom's mother and father were delighted when Tom was offered the job at the boatyard. They knew his wage would be very small, but every little bit helped the family to live.

James's father wasn't in a much better position, but his wage was more regular. He worked as a farm labourer for one of the gentlemen farmers in the area. Both boys' mothers stayed home and looked after their houses, cooked, cleaned and made sure the menfolk were fit and able to fulfil their role of bringing in an income.

Both families lived in the same village. Tom's family home was near the seafront. It nestled alongside a tight bunch of other white limewashed tiny cottages that formed a wall of buildings along the seafront. James's parents lived right at the far side of the township in a tied cottage, which belonged to the landowner. All the people who lived in the area knew full well that life was difficult. If you couldn't work you had to rely on begging, or munificent relations or neighbours.

The two boys had worked solidly for the last four weeks without a day off because their employer wanted to get a boat completed for a very good customer. As a thank you he gave the lads the day off work.

Tom and James found a nice soft patch of grass to sit down on. They sat gazing out to sea, squinting as the sun glistened off the surface of the gently rippling ocean.

'That looks like a large ship coming towards us.'

James strained his eyes in the direction his friend was pointing in. As the sailing ship got ever closer to the secluded bay, the two lads could see that the ship had four masts and was under full sail. Men were climbing the rigging in preparation for gathering up the sails. The whole ship was a hive of activity. The masses of dirty white canvas sails were now being furiously tied up onto their relevant spars of the masts. They could hear one or two of the crew shouting orders as the slight breeze carried their voices inland.

'That's a very big ship,' said James. 'I wonder why they are anchoring here and not in the harbour?'

The boys moved further towards the steep cliff edge and lay on their stomachs. The steep rock face down to the beach was over eighty feet high. There were one or two difficult pathways down to the white-sand beach below, but only a local or a fool would use these to descend to the sea. The clanking sound of the anchor was heard as it was lowered into the sea.

The boys gazed down onto the flurry of activity aboard the vessel. 'Look, the ship has gun ports down its sides. It doesn't look like a Royal Navy ship to me.'

Tom nodded his agreement. 'Who are they?' he asked in reply.

'I think it is some people who don't want to be seen. Otherwise they would have docked into the port,' responded James. The bay was on the far side of the promontory of Compass Point Head. Some two miles away on the opposite side was the little harbour town of Kingsport, where the Bascombe and Purdy families lived.

As the two lads lay as concealed as possible on the cliff top, activity on the ship increased. A large, rough-looking sailor was shouting orders at some of the crew. He had dark, unkempt hair, which was tied in a ponytail. A horizontally striped shirt-like garment, black seamen's three-quarter-length trousers and calf-length black boots made up his dress. The other members of the crew that were visible to Tom and James were also dressed shabbily but serviceably.

'Look down the side of the ship. They have a hole above the water line.' The timbers around the gaping hole were all splintered and smashed. It was about six feet above the water line, so there wasn't any fear of taking on seawater and capsizing.

'That hole hasn't been made by crashing into something. I say that was caused by a cannonball,' said Tom. 'There's something suspicious about that ship and its crew, and I think we should find out more.'

'I think so, but we must be careful,' replied his friend.

A tall man with fair hair emerged from the living quarters of the vessel and stepped out onto the main deck. He was dressed in a short red jacket with gold-coloured buttons and a white cravat about his neck, with dark trousers and shiny black boots. He had a broad leather belt around his waist, which supported a scabbard that held a fearsome-looking curved sabre-like sword. 'I bet he's the captain,' said James.

A rowing boat was now being lowered over the side into the water. As it touched the sea, some of the crew threw a rope ladder down towards the small boat. Six of the crew scrambled down the rope ladder and into the boat. They pushed away from the sailing ship and began rowing towards the beach.

'Oh! They are going to land on the beach below us,' whispered Tom.

About a hundred yards from where they lay was an outcrop of rock standing higher than the grassed area they currently occupied. 'Quick, crawl up to those rocks. We'll have a bit better view, and if they climb up here they won't see us.'

As the boys scrambled to the shelter of the rocky outcrop the small crew of men was fast approaching the silver sands. All six men were well armed with broadswords and two pistols each. If they met any trouble, they would be more than ready.

Chapter 2

Tom and James watched from their hiding place in the crevices of the rocks as the men searched the bottom of the rock face, looking for an access to the top of the cliff face. 'What do you think they are looking for?' whispered James. Tom shrugged his shoulders.

Below one of the men called to his colleagues, 'Over here, mateys, there seems to be a bit of a pathway. It's steep, but it'll be better than breaking out the ropes and climbing.' His shipmates ambled over to observe his discovery.

'Oh, hell's bells, that path will lead them to within a few yards of us,' said Tom in a low voice.

'We're only assuming that they are bad men. They may not be,' responded his friend.

Tom didn't share his friend's optimism: 'Normal people don't go around armed to the teeth.'

It didn't take the men long to climb the steep path to the cliff top. Soon they were standing within a few yards of where Tom and James were hiding.

'I don't know where Cap'n Smyth thinks we might get oak from up here to repair the ship,' grumbled one of the men.

'Use your head, Jack, find some oak trees and cut them down. Throw them down onto the beach, and off we go back to the *Pegasus*.'

Tom's foot slipped on some loose scree. The small

rock fragments rolled away down the slope and out into the open. 'What's that?' exclaimed the bosun. Two of the men scuttled over to where the noise came from. 'Well, well, look what we've found.'

The crewmen dragged the two lads from their hiding place. Silas, the bosun, walked over to the two lads, now securely held by his two crewmen. 'What are you two doing about here? Are you spying on us?'

Tom gave a quick glance at James, who looked as scared as Tom was feeling. 'No sir, we are not spying. It's our day's rest from the boatyard where we work, and we came up here onto the cliff top to enjoy the day.'

'In that case, why were you hiding from us?'

'We were scared sir, honest,' intervened James.

Silas scratched his head. 'I don't see why.'

Tom decided to diffuse the situation. 'It was the pistols and swords that scared us, sir.'

The bosun laughed. 'We only use them on our enemies. Not young boys. You say you work at a boatyard?'

'Yes sir,' replied Tom.

'So the boatyard would have supplies of oak beams and planks?'

'Oh, yes sir. Mr Archer would happily sell you some timber.'

The bosun took his sword belt off and handed his pistols to one of his men. 'I am going into the village with these two youngsters to see their Mr Archer. You lot get back to the ship and inform the Captain what I'm up to.' His men acknowledged his command and headed back towards the cliff top. 'Come on young'uns let's go and see if we can do some trade with your boss. My name is Silas.'

The huge bosun set off down the grassy hillside with Tom on one side of him and James on the other.

'Why do you need some oak, sir?'

Silas glanced at Tom and said, 'Had a bit of an accident with the ship. Put a hole in one side of the *Pegasus*, it did. So before we put back to sea we need a repair.'

Half an hour later the trio wandered into Kingsport boatyard.

'Hello lads, can't you stay away from work for a full day?' said a ruddy-faced Mr Archer.

Silas intervened, 'I met these two lads o'yours up on the cliff top. I'm looking for some oak planks to repair my ship. They told me they might be able to help me out. So here we are.'

Old Mr Archer looked straight into Silas's eyes. 'Depends what you want. But we have plenty of different sizes. More to the point, where's your ship?'

'Ah, that's the problem. I managed to get her to the shelter of the bay on the other side of the headland, but I daren't be thinking of moving her till I get the repair done.'

Archer appeared to accept the man's answer. 'Come with me. I'll show you what we have.'

One hour later the deal had been done. Silas had the timber he needed and had persuaded Mr Archer to cart his purchase on a flat-decked boat he kept at the boatyard around to the *Pegasus*.

'Are these two lads any good at repairing ships?'

Mr Archer smiled and looked fondly at the two lads. 'Best apprentices I have.'

'Would you be good enough to let me borrow them for a couple of days to help me repair my ship?'

'Only two days, mind. Is that all right with you

9

two?' Tom and James nodded their agreement to the deal. Silas and Archer shook hands.

'Be at the beach just after sunrise in the morning and one of my men will be there to row you to the *Pegasus*.'

The following morning the two friends met near Tom's house and walked through the village towards the cliff top. 'I hope we can do the work they want doing. There's something about that ship that makes me uneasy,' said Tom.

'Me too,' replied his friend.

They made their way up the long grassy slope to the cliff edge. At the top they stopped and gazed down into the serene bay. The large sailing ship was still at anchor, all its sails rolled up tightly to their respective yards. As they looked immediately down onto the beach below, they saw a small rowboat pulled partly up onto the soft sand with a lone crewman standing by the side of the boat. The pair scrambled down the steep cliff path. Small rocks, gravel and dust following their unsteady feet. The lads completed their descent and landed on the white sand beach then scrambled across to where the man and his boat were awaiting them.

'Morning,' said James. Tom just smiled at the man who nodded his head and beckoned for them to get into the boat. With his two charges aboard, he pushed the craft off the sand and jumped aboard. He edged himself into position, pulled the oars into a rowing position and began navigating the boat away from the shore and out into the bay. His face was very weatherbeaten. His black straggly unkempt hair was in the first stages of greying. He had a dirty striped shirt made from some heavy-duty material. His dark trousers were shiny with wear. His bare arms had been tattooed extensively. Tom shuddered at the thought of being the man's enemy.

A while later they were pulling alongside the *Pegasus*. A rope ladder was awaiting the trio's ascent. On board, Tom and James couldn't help staring at the spectacle of their surroundings. It was the first time either of them had been aboard such a large vessel. They saw many barrels stacked on the deck. There seemed to be endless quantities of ropes all over the deck, coiled in bundles. Lots of crewmen appeared to be busy carrying out cleaning of rigging and decks. Some were sewing canvas with huge needles.

'Ahoy there, mates,' came a booming voice. Tom and James looked to where the voice was coming from. It was Silas standing up on the rear deck. He waved them to join him. They climbed the companionway stair and walked towards the big man. 'Have you eaten today?'

'No,' said Tom.

'Me neither,' said James.

'Right, follow me. We'll get you fed before you start work.'

Two metal plates full of bread and cheese along with a jug of water were brought to the boys in the galley. As they sat devouring the food, the light shining through the galley doorway was suddenly blocked out. A tall, fair-haired man clad in a white blouse-like shirt, dark trousers and knee-length black shiny boots was standing in the doorway. 'So these two whippets are your boat builders, eh, Silas?'

'Yes, Captain. They be the boat owner's best apprentices.'

Tom and James stared open-mouthed at the tall man,

who strolled over to them and placed one of his feet onto the form where James was sitting. This was the man they had seen yesterday standing near the steering gear, the man in the red jacket with gold buttons.

'This is our captain. Captain Smyth. These two lads be Tom and James.'

The fair-haired man nodded his recognition to Silas. Both lads stood up and thought it polite to introduce themselves properly. 'I'm Tom Bascombe, and this is my friend James Purdy.'

'Pleased to meet you. Do you think you will be able to repair my ship?'

'Sir, we have yet to have a close look at it. But we'll do the best we can.' The captain seemed satisfied and strode out into the sunshine.

With their meal finished, the two lads and Silas went out into the sunshine and made their way towards the front of the ship to view their repair task.

'I have a couple of useful lads who will be able to help you do the work. They are not shipwrights, but they may be able to help you.' Silas spotted his two helpers. 'Ben, John.' He waved the men over and went on to explain what the lads were about to do and instructed them to assist them as best they could.

The two men gave a curled hand form of salute and said, 'Aye aye, bosun.'

'What about tools?' asked Tom.

'We have some shipwrights' tools. Ben and John will get them for you. Down in the forward locker you'll find them, Ben.'

As the two crewmen went away for the tools Tom and James studied the damage and searched amongst the oak timber that had been placed near the repair site. Minutes later the crewmen were back with an assortment of tools.

12

'What caused this damage?' asked James.

'Cannonball,' replied John. His mate nudged him hard. John took the hint and shut up.

'Aye, the lads were having a bit of practice with the deck cannon. Cap'n were furious.'

Tom thought he saw Ben wink at John as he gave the explanation.

All day the lads laboured hard, cutting, shaping and fixing the new timberwork into place. The two crewmen hauled various timbers into place and made the work as easy as possible. Silas made sure the lads were fed and watered. He seemed more than satisfied at their progress.

As twilight was starting, Silas approached Tom and James. 'We can either take you back to the beach, or you can stay aboard for the night.'

James looked at Tom. 'I told my mother I might not get finished today, so I'm all right staying.'

'Me too,' answered Tom.

'Cook is about ready with the men's meal, so down to the galley with both of you.' After a meal of cooked salt beef and vegetables and a tankard of crude ale, the boys went back up on deck and sat looking up at a darkening sky. 'I'm full to bursting. These crewmen get well looked after,' said Tom.

'I'm wondering what sort of trade they do,' responded James.

Before they had chance to ponder on the subject, Silas and a few of the crew came up onto the deck and sat with the two. One of the men pulled a Jew's harp from his pocket, put it to his lips and began playing. More of the crew joined them, and before long a sort of crude concert was set in motion.

13

When Tom and James indicated that they were tired and wished to sleep, Silas motioned a crewman to take them down to their makeshift sleeping space. 'Ever slept on a hammock before?' he asked. Tom and James said they hadn't.

After the man had left them Tom told James he was going to have a look round the lower decks. James grinned and motioned he would go with him. They moved as noiselessly as possible through the ship. Somewhere in the middle of the ship they opened up a wooden bulkhead door and stood speechless. There were lots of big cannons on both sides of the long room. The middle of the floor had barrels tied together. Alongside the barrels were hundreds of cannonballs. All the cannons were facing closed trapdoors in each side of the ship, which when opened, the cannons could be pushed out to fire at enemy ships.

'There are twelve cannons on each side of the ship. Twenty-four guns doesn't make it a merchant ship to my mind,' said a shocked James.

'What kind of ship is this?' responded Tom to his friend's look of incredulity.

'A pirate ship.'

The two lads whirled round to discover who had answered their query. Standing in the bulkhead doorway was Captain Smyth.

'I thought you had been instructed to go to your hammocks when you retired. You weren't expected to go nosing around the *Pegasus*. Silas employed you to repair the damage to the side and then go back to your jobs.'

'But sir, we only wanted to look around your ship.'

'That look around may have cost you your freedom,' replied the captain.

14

Tom was now in a half protesting, half pleading mode. 'But sir, we promised our families and our employer that as soon as we finish your job we will be home.'

'And so you would have been if you had not decided to satisfy your curiosity and discover things you had no business in interfering with. We sailed into this bay as secretly as possible just to get the repair done quietly and without anyone knowing. Unfortunately for you, Silas came across you two and discovered that you knew something about shipbuilding. It's a real pity, because you are two very able and likeable lads. In the short time I have come to know you I have taken a shine to you.'

James was getting really upset now. 'Are you going to kill us?'

Smyth laughed out loud. 'No, don't be silly. We don't go around killing boys. I want you to finish the repair and then we will sail out to sea. If we find somewhere quiet around the south coast we will drop you off in one of our small boats and leave you on a beach somewhere.'

Tom and James looked at each other with some relief on their faces. 'But sir, how will we get back home?' asked Tom.

'That will be for you to decide.' Now I suggest you get some sleep. Tomorrow will be a busy day for you.'

The two friends slept very little that night. What did the future hold for them?

Chapter 3

The morning brought another beautiful day. The sun cast its glow across the rigging of the magnificent ship. Silas must have been instructed by the captain to keep a wary eye on Tom and James, as two more of the crew had been assigned to assist them as well as the helpers they had the day before.

The boys were given breakfast before the day's labours began. Tom and James knew full well that any chance of escape would be futile and most likely end in their death. They resolved to get the task finished and then rely on the generosity of the captain to free them as he had promised.

The sun was just beginning its nightly descent below the skyline when the two exhausted lads stood back and proclaimed the repair of the ship's side completed. Silas came over to cast his eye over the job. 'Credit to you, boys, that is a real good job befitting a qualified shipwright. Stay here, you two, I'll fetch the cap'n.' With that he strode over to the rear of the ship, where the captain's living quarters were.

A few minutes later Captain Smyth and Silas were heading towards the two boys. Smyth inspected the work thoroughly and stood looking at the lads when he had examined their work. 'That seems to be a seaworthy job. I thank you lads very much. We shall

16

see that you get fed like princes.' He dipped his hand into a pouch hanging off his belt and produced two gold coins, handing a coin to each boy. Tom and James just looked at the glistening gold coins. Neither of them had had a gold sovereign before.

'Tomorrow we set sail, and true to our bargain, we shall find somewhere safe for us to row you to land and then you can make your way home.'

Tom and James put their money away safely into inner pockets and followed Silas down to the galley. The captain had not been joking when he told them they would eat royally. After a wonderful feast, all washed down with crude ale, they could not have cared less whether they were on a pirate ship or any other ship; sleep was the only thing on their minds. They climbed up into their hammocks, and seconds later they were fast asleep.

'Tom, wake up. We're moving. Wake up.' Bleary-eyed, Tom responded to the shaking. Everything was swaying about. They jumped down from their hammocks and rushed up onto the main deck. It was a cloudy day but fine. Land was a distant line on the horizon.

'James, we're miles from land. I wonder if we will ever see home again.'

'Top o' the morning to 'ee lads,' chirped a happy Silas.

'Morning, sir,' they responded.

A gentle breeze was filling the sails. All three masts were now hidden, with the masses of sail canvas billowing out, accepting the wind.

'Where are we sailing to?' asked Tom.

'Oh, don't worry your heads, lads, the cap'n will drop you off somewhere.' With that Silas shouted some urgent orders to some nearby crewmen and marched off towards them.

The two made their way up onto the poop deck to chat with the seaman at the wheel. As he was steering the ship, he must know where they were heading.

The sailor smiled as they approached. 'Where are we going, sir?' The seaman smiled again and said, 'East.' James looked at Tom with a look that said 'That's not an answer'.

Tom estimated that they had now been sailing further away from land for over an hour; unfortunately he wasn't sure of their true direction, nor was he sure of the time. Men went about their everyday tasks on the open decks and below decks.

A shrill whistle pierced the air. 'Ships to port.' A crewman high in the top rigging was calling out for his superiors to hear him.

Silas found a telescope and put it to his eye. At that very moment Captain Smyth emerged from his quarters, armed with his own telescope. Silas hurried over to his captain. 'I spot eight ships yonder,' he said.

'So do I. Two of them appear to be British, but the other six seem to be flying another flag. Tell the helmsman to get a bit closer. Not too close, mind.'

A while later the *Pegasus* had drawn a little nearer to the spread-out group of ships. 'There's trouble ahead,' said Smyth as he again put his telescope to his eye.

Silas followed his master's actions. 'Those other six ships are Spanish. They'll attempt to sink the two British man-o-war ships. We can't afford to get mixed up in their fight,' he said with a querying look in his eyes.

'Silas, my boy, if you think for one moment that we are going to sail away and let good British sailors meet their Davy Jones, you will be disappointed. Haul up the Union Jack.'

'Aye, aye, sir.' With that, Silas dashed off to organise battle stations.

Captain Smyth saw the two apprentices standing at the rear of the poop deck. He strode over to them. 'It will get very dangerous for you to stay up here soon. You should go below decks.'

'Sir, why are Spanish ships attacking British Navy ships?' asked Tom.

'It's all to do with a piece of land many miles away called Gibraltar. The Spanish reckon it should belong to them but currently we occupy it. The Spanish Government has ordered its navy to attack British shipping, and British frigates taken or sunk would be a real feather in a Spanish captain's cap.'

Tom and James had a puzzled frown on their faces. 'I can see another question here,' said Smyth.

'Well, sir, you are pirates and you wish to help the British Navy. I would have thought you would have sailed away in the opposite direction,' responded James.

'Firstly, we have never attacked or raided any ship flying a British flag. Secondly, we don't like the Spanish, as they would happily sink us given half a chance.'

The captain was now anxious to get ready for the upcoming fight, so he said to the boys, 'When this fight is over I will tell you a little bit about myself and some of my crew.' With that he sped away to his cabin.

All the crew was rushing around in an orderly fashion, preparing for the coming battle. Gun ports were opened up on both sides of the vessel, and cannons were now protruding from the openings. Some of the huge sails were gathered in to reduce the contact speed of the ship.

Captain Smyth emerged from his quarters dressed in an immaculate three-quarter-length coat decorated with shiny brass buttons. His knee-length boots looked as though they had received an extra special polish. He now wore a large tricorn hat. At his waist he wore a wide black belt holding a cutlass and two large pistols. The two lads couldn't help but admire the style of the man.

He spotted the boys. 'I told you, go below to my cabin and look out of the windows. Now, go.' Tom and James hurried away to the captain's quarters.

The British and Spanish ships were now closing in on each other. Cannons were being fired from all the ships and the air was full of gunsmoke. Tom tapped James on the shoulder to see what he was looking at. A British man-o-war had fired a low-level salvo into the side of one of the Spanish ships. This had torn away a good deal of the ship's side and the ship had rapidly taken on water. The big vessel lurched over on its side with the result that its cannons slid to the damaged side of the vessel, making its stability even more precarious. The huge rip in the side was now under the water line and the ship began to sink rapidly. Spanish sailors leaped over the side of the ship into the sea.

The other British ship was further away from the action and firing at some distance. Two Spanish warships were manoeuvring themselves onto the rear end of the British ship, away from its deadly cannonade. Captain Smyth saw what was happening and directed the *Pegasus* to speed to the aid of the man-o-war.

The *Pegasus* drew down alongside one of the Spanish ships and at the same time released a full salvo of cannonballs into the Spanish ship. The twelve cannon balls couldn't help but find their mark at such close range. Practically the whole side of the enemy ship disintegrated into splintered fragments of wood, most of which floated in the sea.

The British ship began to turn so that it could use its cannons more effectively. The Spanish ship released a cannonade at the man-o-war and felled its rear mast and Smyth manoeuvred his ship to the rear of the British frigate and now had a full side target at the enemy. 'Fire,' he commanded. The *Pegasus* rocked as all the guns on one side of the ship were triggered at once. The huge cannonballs ripped through the enemy vessel like a hot knife cutting butter. The ship immediately lurched over and began to sink. Men on the British ship began to cheer their helpers. Captain Smyth acknowledged the cheering by standing up on the rear of his ship and waving his cocked hat in appreciation. 'Turn about; we still have three more of them to sort out.'

Now it was an even fight. Three British, fighting three Spanish. The other British ship was heavily engaged in battling the remaining Spaniards. A mast was missing on one Spanish vessel and the rear top corner of the deck was blown away on the British ship. The *Pegasus* and the man-o-war hurried to assist the beleaguered British ship. As the first Spanish ship drew close, the captains of both the Navy ship and the *Pegasus* seemed to operate as one man: the guns of both ships seemed to fire at the same time. One of the Spanish ships appeared to disintegrate into the sea as Tom and James stared in disbelief at the spectacle. The reaction from the tremendous broadside of cannon fire lurched the ship so violently that they fell over onto the cabin floor. The ship was now heading towards one of the two Spanish ships left in the fight. A crunching, bone-shattering bang resonated through the whole vessel as the *Pegasus* collided with one of the enemy ships.

Instantly Captain Smyth and his men used their own ship's ropes and rigging to hurl themselves onto the large Spanish ship. Pistol and muskets were being fired at anything that moved. Both sides were firing into the enemy's ranks. Men were falling all over, most covered in blood. Smyth's crew were squealing at the tops of their voices. The sounds put fear into Tom and James. What affect it had on their enemies, the boys could only imagine.

The *Pegasus*'s crew cut and chopped their way to an eventual victory. The Spanish captain hurriedly produced a piece of white material and waved it above his head. He was surrendering. Smyth shouted at full voice, 'No more killing.' Everyone dramatically came to a halt as though a spell had been cast upon both sides. Smyth's crew began to collect all the enemies' weapons and transport them to his own ship.

One of the British Navy frigates pulled alongside the Spanish ship. The captain and his officers and most of the crew craned over the side to see the state of the ship and its defeated crew. 'Well done, sir,' cried the British captain. Smyth smiled and acknowledged the compliment with a wave. 'Permission to come aboard and shake your hand, sir.'

Smyth again smiled. 'We can do better than that, sir. I think a strong drink is in order.'

The two ships' masters shook hands aboard the *Pegasus* and sat down in the captain's cabin with supplies of rum and wine. The British officer introduced himself as Post Captain Duncannon of His Majesty's Royal Navy. Smyth simply introduced himself as Jonathan Smyth.

'Tell me, sir, you are obviously not a merchantman with such a large commitment of cannons and other weapons. May I enquire if you are a privateer?' (A privateer was a ship and crew holding a Government commission who were authorised to attack and capture hostile shipping for the Government's benefit.)

Smyth did not smile at the question. A querying look drifted across his face. The Post Captain realised he might have touched a sore point. 'Come, sir, you have nothing to fear from me or my crew. The service you have given to His Majesty's Navy this day needs rewarding.'

The semblance of Smyth's familiar grin reappeared on his face. 'You might say that in the loosest of terms, sir.'

'It is as I guessed,' said Duncannon. 'You would be better described as a pirate. The way your crew leaped aboard the Spanish ship and savaged the enemy went far beyond that of a disciplined naval crew. As I say, you have nothing to fear from us. If it had not been for your timely intervention this day, we might not be having this conversation. We could have been either captured or lying at the bottom of the sea. Instead we have only a few casualties, and the bonus is, we now have two Spanish ships practically intact to take home as fortunes of war.'

Smyth smiled his gratitude and thanked Duncannon. 'A pirate I may be, but I can assure you, sir, I have never attacked or robbed any British vessel.'

Duncannon poured himself another glass of wine. 'I believe you. In my experience, renegade pirates would have waited out of gunshot range to pick over the bones of the fight after it was finished and taken the spoils for themselves.'

'Would you like some food, Captain? My men will be eating, why not us also?'

'Should we be formal with each other? My name is James.'

'And I am Jonathan.' He rang the little bell on his table to signal his orderly and order food. 'Find me Tom and James. They may as well eat with us too.' The orderly gave his master the customary curled-fingered salute to his forehead and went off to carry out his orders.

A while later the orderly returned with food and the two boys, also carrying trays of food. 'Let me introduce you to my two young friends, James.'

'May I be impertinent and ask why you became a pirate, Jonathan?'

'It is rather a long story, but if you have the time, I am prepared to tell you. I had promised my young friends the same story anyway.' Duncannon said he would be honoured to hear his new friend's tale.

Jonathan Smyth settled himself into his chair and began his story. 'I was the only son born to a baronet. He was lord of the manor of Credlington in the county of Devon. After he died of old age I inherited both his title and his house and lands. Probably because of his age and failing health, the house and the management of the estate were suffering. I discovered he had big debts. I enlisted the help of various experts to set the estate back on a path of prosperity.

'Over a number of years my hard work with the help of my loyal staff paid dividends. We planted more new trees than we cut down and became one of the chief foresters in the county. We increased the cattle and sheep stock tenfold. We became the primary source of livestock for many miles around. I managed to pay off all my father's debts and discovered that we had a surplus of funds left over. I then decided to start a farmers' bank. As the local farmers collected monies for their produce, instead of keeping the money at home with risk of thieves stealing their money, they would bring it to our bank. After a few years we became so successful that we had four branches in different parts of the county. Suddenly I was a very wealthy man. Looking back, that is where my troubles began.'

Duncannon interrupted him. 'I don't see how becoming a wealthy man can bring on trouble.'

'Believe me, my friend, it can.' Duncannon smiled broadly at Jonathan referring to him as friend.

Jonathan resumed his story. 'I was practically brought up with a boy on the neighbouring estate to ours. Their property wasn't as large as ours, but with both our fathers being good friends it was inevitable that the two of us should be friends. This situation prevailed through boyhood and into manhood. We were practically inseparable. When my father and mother died he grieved for me, and likewise when his parents passed away I grieved with him. As the time passed and I became successful, he began to become more distant from me. Eventually I met a beautiful woman. After some months we married.

'I later discovered my friend had wanted to eventually marry the woman I had married. We became even more distant from each other. He began to spread rumours that I was cheating the farmers with their bank accounts. I eventually reverted to the course of law to stop him making false accusations against my business and me. Lawyers issued him with letters stating that if he did not withdraw his false accusations against me, he would be held to account in a court of law. Jealousy and hate had now replaced what was once an inseparable friendship. He was jealous of my success and of my marriage.

'I had to travel to London on business, which took me most of a week to go there and back and conclude my business. On returning back home, my household staff ran out to greet me, despair written all over their faces. They told me that some masked men had abducted my wife. They came in the middle of the night and broke into the house, ran upstairs and wrapped my wife in her bedclothes and attempted to make their getaway without any noise. My butler heard the commotion and ran from his bed. My wife managed to get one arm free and wrenched the mask off the face of the man nearest to her head. My butler told me it was my old friend who was the abductor.'

'Good gad, sir!' was Duncannon's exclamation.

Smyth pressed on with his tale. 'We saddled up fresh horses, and some of my youngest staff and myself set off across country to find her. We arrived at my one-time friend's house to discover he had gone away with my wife. With threats of violence we interrogated his staff to tell us where he was in hiding. Eventually they told us where he might be. He had a cottage hidden away in the woods some ten miles away.

'We made our way there as quickly as we could. We tied up the horses some yards from the house and stealthily crept towards the cottage. We quietly walked round the building till we found a loosely latched window, and one of my staff then climbed

26

inside. The rest of us continued to survey the building, as every window seemed to be in darkness. One of my staff discovered that horses were tied up in the stables at the back of the house. From that we assumed that people were present in the building. Suddenly an anguished cry emanated from inside. Two of us climbed in through the open window to be met by two burly men. We fought with them. I managed to plunge my dagger into one of them, at which he fell to the floor writhing. My colleague had pulled out his pistol and fired into the other man's chest. The sound was deafening. We then heard feet scurrying up the corridor and, seconds later, another blood-curdling cry.

'Rushing towards the corridor, we tripped over a body. It was the member of my staff who had initially climbed through the window. He was dead. Glass was being broken. Someone was smashing windows. I found a small lantern and lit it so that we could see where we were going. My colleague found another lantern and we now had enough light to find our way about the place. We then came across another room at the far end of the corridor.

'As I pushed open the door my senses went into a spin. I could not comprehend what my eyes were seeing. My wife was tied up in a chair and her head was lying to one side. The whole front of her dress was covered in blood. I rushed over to her and realised that she was dead. She had been viciously stabbed. I could not contain my rage and despair. One of my staff had broken down the door and came in to inform me that the gang had made a getaway using the horses from the stables. He told me that one of the men was my former friend. I instructed them to follow them. The fight had gone from me.

I collapsed onto the floor, absolutely distraught.' Listening to this sorry tale were Tom and James and James Duncannon. All three sat open mouthed with disbelief.

'This is the most awful tale I have ever heard. I cannot express my sorrow that I feel for what you have suffered,' said Duncannon.

'It did not end there.'

Duncannon's mouth dropped open. 'You suffered further?'

'Oh, yes. I mourned my murdered wife. My staff could not find the gang and my former friend. About a month later, the sheriff sent some of his constables to my house. I wasn't at home when they came, so they asked my butler when I would be at home. He asked them what they wanted. They told him they had come to arrest me for the murder of my wife and my former friend's colleague.

My butler told the constables a lie. He told them I would not be back home for two days as I was in London on business. In actual fact I was in another part of the county and was due home by the evening. Johnson, my faithful butler, knew that I had not had any part in my wife's tragic death. He knew I had tried to save her.

'When he told me of the day's events later that evening, I became enraged and full of revenge, a feeling I had never experienced since my wife's death. Johnson eventually calmed me and made me listen to reason. He told me that I couldn't prove it wasn't me who had killed her and that my one-time friend would be probably believed if he swore against me in court. Johnson spoke a lot of sense. I decided there and then to make my escape and go into hiding

28

until I could prove my innocence and my former friend's guilt for his dastardly deeds.

'We collected together all the money, gold and valuables I had in the house, and ordered two of my most trusted staff to saddle up fresh horses. Johnson swore he would look after the estate until I returned. He was used to dealing with my various managers when I had been away, so I had no misgivings about his loyalty. The two staff asked if they could accompany me on my escape. So it was that a few hours later the three of us escaped into the night, not knowing what fate lay ahead of us.

'For six months we rented various houses and cottages and lived as far away from the law as possible. Then one day we arrived in Portsmouth and the idea came to me that we would be the safest if we lived at sea. I bought the *Pegasus*, acquired a crew, and piracy was the next step on my miserable demise. Silas and Preston are the two trusted staff that have stayed with me. I regret that I have turned them into outlaws as well as myself.'

He sat back in his armchair, looked at his audience and said, 'That is the end of my sorry tale.'

Tom and James sat with open mouths, not being able to believe all that they had heard. James Duncannon just whistled through his teeth. 'Jonathan, I cannot believe that you have suffered such misfortune and damnable fate. I would deem it an honour if I could assist you in any way to get your freedom, lands and property restored to you.'

'Why, I thank you very much for your kindness, James. I don't doubt that I need some influential help, and if you could assist me in any way I will remain eternally grateful to you.'

Duncannon looked up at the cabin ceiling and

thought of what he could do to help his new friend. Eventually he said, 'I have naval leave due to me. I think we should use the time wisely and rescue your honour.'

Chapter 4

The three ships rested at anchor that night along with the captured Spanish ships. The following day, James Duncannon told Jonathan Smyth that he would be sailing his tiny fleet back to Portsmouth, to the naval dockyard. 'I shall make it in my way, through my superiors, that the King be notified of you and your crew's gallant action in achieving the victory that we have all gained. Furthermore, I intend to seek a pardon for all of you.'

Jonathan Smyth thanked Duncannon and wished him a safe journey. Tom and James approached Captain Smyth. 'Sir, where exactly do you intend landing us?'

Smyth looked at the two boys. The broad smile returned to his face. 'I think, Tom, and you, James, that our fortunes have changed since last we spoke about where we were setting you down. Up to yesterday, we were all wanted men. It now appears that James Duncannon may be able to procure us a pardon. I therefore think that we should risk sailing back to the bay at Kingsport. There one of my crew will row you back to the beach.'

Tom and James were delighted and shook the captain's hands. He drew them to him and said, 'You are both brave lads and we thank you for your hard work. Without your help, we wouldn't have been able to assist James Duncannon and his men in defeating those Spaniards.'

Tom looked towards his friend and then at the captain. 'Sir, do you think we will be able to assist you in seeking out your friend turned enemy and helping you get your estates back?'

'I think that part of my future could be very dangerous. It may be better for you not to be involved.'

The two looked really disappointed at Smyth's words. He recognised the look, smiled again and said, 'Well, we shall have to see in what way you will be able to help me.' He then shouted, 'Silas, make the ship ready. We sail for the bay at Kingsport.'

'Aye, aye, sir.'

The *Pegasus* was now in full sail and making its way west.

The following day Tom and James went up on deck to find a familiar sight. In the distance they could see the cliffs of Kingsport, which were getting nearer by the minute. A few hours later the ship dropped anchor in the quiet bay and a rowing boat was lowered over the side. Tom and James said their farewells to the crew and lastly to Captain Smyth. 'When I need your help, I will send Silas to fetch you. He will come to the boatyard.' Tom and James climbed down into the little boat and wondered whether they would ever see the charismatic captain again. The crewman rowed them to the beach, bid them farewell and returned to his ship. 'Life is going to be dull from now on,' said James.

They reached the cliff top, stood and stared out to sea. The sails were being lowered on the *Pegasus* and she was moving steadily back out to sea. The pair waved at the ship. Captain Smyth, Silas and a few of the crew stood at the rear of the ship and waved. Under full sail the *Pegasus* caught the wind and accelerated away into the overcast morning. Tom and James began making up the stories they would tell their parents as they trudged down the grassy slope towards the town.

A month passed by before a courier arrived at the naval dockyard with a message for Post Captain James Duncannon. He hurriedly opened the letter, which bore an admiral's seal. As he read, his smile began to get broader. His captain was beside him. 'Good news, sir?'

'The best, the King has granted Jonathan Smyth a Royal Pardon. The only problem is that he is required to go to the palace to promise the King in person that he will never stray outside the law again.'

'Sorry, sir, but how is that a problem?'

'We have to find him to tell him. That is the problem.'

Over the following days, Duncannon in his quest to locate the *Pegasus* alerted all navy vessels to signal any sightings. It was six weeks before any word of a sighting was received. A lieutenant knocked loudly on Duncannon's land-based office door. 'Sir, we have had a sighting of the *Pegasus*. It was seen in the Bay of Biscay.'

'Good, what steps have we made to contact the ship?'

'It will have been made by now, sir. It all happened over two days ago. I can only anticipate that our ship intercepted the *Pegasus* and asked it to sail to Portsmouth.'

Duncannon had a look of satisfaction and success on his face. 'Thank you lieutenant, keep me informed.' The officer saluted and left.

* * *

Out in the Bay of Biscay the Royal Navy ship *Warrior* had sent a flag signal to the crew of the *Pegasus*, requesting that they pull alongside to hear news for their captain. Smyth held his telescope to his eye and immediately instructed the helmsman to bring the ship alongside the *Warrior*. As grappling irons secured the two ships together, the true extent of their differing sizes became apparent, the enormous Navy frigate, *Warrior*, dwarfed the *Pegasus*. Silas looked up towards the deck of the Navy frigate and said to the crew surrounding him, 'I am glad this meeting is a friendly one. They could easily blow us out of the water with just a few of their guns.' A rope ladder was thrown onto the *Pegasus* to enable Jonathan Smyth to climb aboard the Navy ship.

Once on board, he was directed to the captain's cabin. The captain extracted a sheet of paper and handed it to Smyth. 'By order of the King you have been ordered to sail back to England,' he said as he handed the document to Smyth. It was a short note from Duncannon informing him about the King's pardon and the conditions he had attached.

'Thank you, Captain, I will do as ordered and sail immediately home.'

The captain was not impressed. 'I understand you are a pirate. I thought we hanged pirates.'

Smyth was not going to be rattled by this man. 'Maybe so, sir. There are good pirates and bad pirates. Thank you for delivering the message.' With that he turned on his heel, opened the cabin door and disappeared out onto the deck.

Back on board his ship Smyth ordered his crew to make full sail and head for England.

* * *

34

Three days later the *Pegasus* was edging its way into the naval dock at Portsmouth. As the ship was anchored, Duncannon strode out onto the dockside to await Smyth coming ashore. The two shook hands. 'Good to see you again, Jonathan.'

'And you, James.'

'I have organised a bed for you in the officers' quarters, and tomorrow we ride to London,' said Duncannon.

The following day, a carriage with four horses set off for London with Duncannon and Jonathan Smyth aboard. When the audience with the King had been arranged, the two men were summoned to the palace. The King informed Smyth of the pardon and told him that he was expected to return to a law-abiding life and set an example to the community in which he lived.

'Sire, before I can make you such a promise I have to right an injustice and seek vengeance for the death of my wife.'

The King scowled at Smyth. 'I have heard briefly of the unfortunate situation which has befallen you. But I must warn you that if you attempt to take the law into your own hands, the pardon will be withdrawn and you will be tried as a criminal. I advise you to seek any recourse within the realms of the law.'

Smyth bowed deeply. 'Thank you, sire. I hereby give you my word.' Both men walked backwards out of the room.

'So what do you intend doing now?' asked Duncannon.

'Firstly, I must return to my ship, release most of

the crew and secure a safe haven for the vessel, then concoct a plan for my immediate future.'

'I trust you still require me to assist you?' asked James Duncannon.

'I wouldn't have it any other way, my friend.'

Captain Jonathan Smyth addressed his crew on the main deck of his ship. 'I have already informed Silas, Preston and Caleb and a few of my other comrades who worked on my estate in the past, of my future intentions. Now I feel it my duty to tell you what lies before me and of my future.'

He went on to tell the crew of the recent events and his pardon from the King. 'I do not intend you to have no future just because I am giving up the sea. Silas and a few of the crew wish to continue with me, but it will not be possible for all of you to travel with me. I therefore intend to give you the *Pegasus* as a gift to continue sailing the high seas, or you may dispose of it and share the proceeds. I must warn you that as a pardon has been given to me and in effect to you my crew, that for you to continue sailing the seven seas as pirates would inevitably bring the full weight of the law on your heads. It would result that if you were caught you would certainly be hanged for piracy. You must therefore think carefully what you intend doing before you again set sail. Finally, I thank you for all your loyalty that you have shown me during our time together and wish you well in the future.' With that Smyth took off his tricorn hat and saluted his men. A cheer went up from the crew.

With all their belongings loaded onto a waiting carriage at the small dockside away from any military ships, Smyth, Silas, Preston, Caleb and two other comrades said their final goodbyes to the crew.

The four large horses pulling the carriage moved

away at a gentle trot from the *Pegasus* and onto the little byway that would lead them back to Credlington Manor.

Only Silas and Caleb sat inside the carriage with Smyth, the other three sat up on the outer seating.

Smyth had previously arranged to make a detour to a small coaching inn some 50 miles away from the naval dockyard to meet Duncannon. The carriage rattled over the cobbles in the coachyard of the inn and drew to a stop. Silas ordered the ostler to release the horses from their reins and feed and water them while Smyth strode into the inn and ordered food and drink for him and his men. 'I wish to enquire if a Captain James Duncannon has arrived here yet?' he asked the landlord.

'No, sir,' was the reply. 'I'll inform him you are here when he does arrive.'

Smyth thanked the man and took his seat at a dining table, awaiting the arrival of the food. When their belongings had been unloaded into their individual rooms, the rest of Smyth's men joined him.

Over their meal Smyth instructed Silas on the duties he had planned for him the following morning. 'Hire two horses from the inn stable, and you and Preston ride to Kingsport. You will have to go to the boatyard and seek out young Tom and James. Don't tell them we need them; just ask if they want to join us. If they wish to come, I will leave it up to you to overcome any problems with their employer.'

It was just before dusk when a lone rider rode into the inn yard, his horse's hooves clattering on the cobbles. The tall, athletic figure of James Duncannon came striding into the inn and announced himself to the landlord. 'Ah, please walk this way, sir, there is a gentleman awaiting you.'

Smyth was sitting alone in a large winged chair with his feet resting on the big fire surround and smoking a clay pipe.

'Jonathan.' On hearing the familiar voice, he leaped to his feet.

'James, my dear friend, how good to see you again. Firstly, I will get you some refreshments.' The two men patted each other and shook hands.

Whilst eating his meal, James asked his friend if he had yet made a plan to retrieve his honour and estates. Jonathan told him what had happened up to date. 'Silas and Preston are riding tomorrow to find Tom and James, and they will meet us at Credlington Manor in two days hopefully.

'I need to establish what is happening at Credlington Manor. I am sure Johnson will have kept a careful eye on things, but if there is any news he will bring me up to date.'

Duncannon nodded in agreement at Smyth's reasoning.

'I think that following what news we discover we should then attempt to find the whereabouts of the rascal Donald Fortyscue.'

'Who is he?' asked Duncannon.

'Ah, sorry. I have never mentioned his name before. He was the man that I used to call my friend and who murdered my wife.'

The two men chatted for a further half hour until Duncannon yawned.

'My dear fellow, I am forgetting you have had a long ride. I shall let you get to bed. We have an early start in the morning.'

After breakfast Smyth collected his belongings and

took them out to the carriage. Minutes later James Duncannon followed him out into the courtyard with his own luggage. 'Silas and Preston left for Kingsport earlier. One of them has taken your horse as we are using the carriage.'

Duncannon smiled. 'It will be a pleasure to ride in the carriage after yesterday's ride.'

Caleb and the other two men decided that they would ride on the top and allow Smyth and Duncannon to chat together inside – after all it was a lovely morning and being sailors they preferred the fresh air.

A few minutes later the horse-drawn carriage clattered across the cobbled yard and out onto the highway eventually taking them to Jonathan Smyth's home.

It was mid-afternoon when Silas and Preston trotted into the village of Kingsport. They guided their horses through the tiny streets towards the boatyard. As they dismounted, the boatyard owner happened to be walking across the yard. He turned to see who had entered the premises. His eyebrows raised, it then came to him. 'Silas, isn't it?'

Silas smiled, 'Nice to see you again, sir.'

'I suppose you need more timber?'

Silas shook his head, 'No, sir, it's more than that.'

A bench was nearby. The owner sat down and indicated the other two men to sit with him. 'If you have a tale to tell, I suggest you begin at the beginning.'

Silas related the whole saga to the man.

'Now, that is a story and no mistake. But how can I help?'

'Well, sir, Captain Smyth did promise Tom and

James that he would contact them once he had been pardoned. They had asked if they could help him regain his honour and bring the villain to justice.'

The big man took his hat off and scratched his grey-haired head. 'The two young 'uns are busy at present. How long will they be away from me?'

Silas exhaled, 'To be honest, sir, I couldn't give you an answer.'

'We had better go and talk to them. Don't forget that even if they say they want to go, they have parents who may not let them.'

Tom and James were busy working away on the skeleton of a fishing boat. 'Tom, James, someone here to see you.'

The two boys looked up from their task. Their faces lit up when they saw Silas, then they jumped out from the timber skeleton and ran over to Silas and Preston. Both boys and Silas had a soft spot for each other; he secretly liked to think that in another world they would have been the sons he never had in this world. He hugged the lads.

An excited Tom spluttered, 'Why are you here? Has anything happened to Captain Smyth?'

'No, no, he is safe and on his way to Credlington Manor with Captain Duncannon.'

The owner gave them permission to sit and chat with each other and walked away to take care of his other duties. Silas sat between the lads, with Preston on the outside of the little group and went through a shortened version of the tale he had related to the boatyard owner. Tom and James sat wide-eyed as they listened.

As Silas completed his story he said, 'So, boys, Captain Smyth has sent us to tell you he is prepared to keep his promise and let you help him regain his honour.'

40

In unison Tom and James said, 'Yes, we want to come with you.'

Silas waved his hands in the air, 'Lads, you have your parents to consider. You can't come with us without their agreement. Preston and I will stay at the Ship Inn tonight, and you talk to your parents and let us know what their decision is. It may be better if they'll put something on paper so I can show Captain Smyth. Now go and ask your employer's permission also.'

The following morning a tousled-haired Tom arrived at the Ship Inn. He was wearing a rough cloth jacket covering an open-necked crude shirt with a neckerchief about his neck. He had three-quarter-length breeches, rough woollen stockings and black leather boots on his feet. Over his shoulder was a canvas sack holding some spare clothing.

'Is your matey James coming?' asked Silas.

'Aye, sir, he should be along soon. He has further to come than me.'

A quarter of an hour later James hurried into the inn, breathless. He was by and large similarly attired to Tom and had his meagre belongings in a sack.

'Sounds like you've been running, Jim. Sit down and get your wind back,' instructed Preston.

'I thought you might have set off without me,' came the breathless reply.

The men finished their clay pipes and then asked the lads if they had permission from their parents. Tom produced a torn scrap of yellowing paper. On it was a few crude words. 'Dad's not good at words but said it's all right for me to help Captain Smyth. Hopes it won't take more'n a month.'

James said, 'My dad can't write, but said it's all right for me to help.'

Silas and Preston smiled at the two lads. 'We have two big strong horses in the stable. If we take it steady we will be able double up on each horse. James can ride with Preston and you with me.' Not long after, the foursome was on the road, the horses striding out proudly in the morning sunshine.

That same morning, Smyth and Duncannon reached the hill overlooking Credlington Manor. The big house lay out before them its front elevation gleaming in the morning sunlight. The carriage rumbled down the slope towards the front entrance. All seemed quiet. 'Just stay up on top with your muskets cocked, men, until I have found that all is well,' ordered Smyth.

Duncannon and Smyth jumped down from the carriage and approached the front door. They each had a cocked pistol. Smyth pushed on the big door and entered quietly. Duncannon stood in the doorway while his friend went further into the entrance hall. Everyone was alert for any problems they might encounter.

Jonathan headed through the house with James staying a distance behind him just in case Smyth was attacked from behind. He pushed open the kitchen door quietly and peered round the kitchen doorway into the cavernous kitchen. Two female servants were trying to conceal themselves in an alcove. When they saw Smyth's face, the relief was plainly visible. 'Oh, sir, praise the Lord that it is you. We heard the wheels over the cobbles and took fright.'

'Tell me, Mary, what have you to be frightened of?'

asked Jonathan. Duncannon now joined his friend. Mary winced when she saw him with the cocked pistol in his hand, standing in the open doorway. 'Don't worry, Mary, this is my friend James Duncannon. There are also some more of my men out with the coach. Now tell me of your concerns.' He ushered Mary and her colleague to sit down.

Mary wiped her hands down her apron, looked at her master and began her tale. 'Well, sir, last night some men came into the house from the back garden. They were armed with swords and pistols. They took hold of Mr Johnson and rough-handled him. They demanded to know where you were. Mr Johnson wouldn't tell them, so they beat him and took him away. So you see, sir, we have been a-hiding since.'

Smyth looked horrified. 'You'll be safe now, Mary. Can you get us all some refreshment? Then we shall see what we can do to get Johnson back safely.'

After a search of the grounds Smyth and his small crew discussed the best strategy for rescuing Johnson. 'Who are Johnson's abductors? And how did they know that you had been pardoned and that you were returning here? And why are they, whoever they are, so anxious to get you?' asked Duncannon.

'A lot of questions there, my friend. I think the answer to the first is they are part of Fortyscue's gang. The rest I cannot answer at the moment.'

'So where do you think we should begin?'

Smyth stroked his chin in thought. 'When Silas and Preston get here we'll split up and ask around the local villages, inns and markets, those kinds of places. Someone will have heard somebody speaking to someone, especially after a few ales.' Duncannon nodded in agreement.

* * *

Just as the sun was beginning to set behind the far hills Caleb ran into the large manor house. 'Captain Jonathan, sir.'

'What is it, Caleb?'

'Two horses coming into the valley, sir. They were just a bit too far away to see who it were.'

'Keep alert, bear in mind it may be Silas and Preston.'

'Aye, aye, sir.' With that Caleb ran back out into the yard to keep watch.

Ten minutes later Silas, Preston and the two boys wearily rode into the manor's front yard. Caleb and his colleagues beamed all over their faces to see their friends again. 'Good to see you and the lads again, Silas. Leave the horses to us, we'll stable them.'

Silas thanked his friend. He stood at the side of his mount and stretched. 'It's been a long time since I spent such a long time astride a horse.' He encouraged the two boys to follow him into the house.

Tom and James had never been in a house as large as this one. Their eyes wandered all round. 'Look at that stairway, it's huge,' exclaimed Tom. James just nodded in awe.

Smyth opened the drawing room door and came out into the large hall. His face broke into a huge smile and he held out his hands in a welcoming gesture. 'It's good to see you again, lads. You all must be exhausted after your long ride here. Mary has prepared you some bread and cold meats, so come and eat heartily.' The boys, Silas and Preston didn't need a second invitation.

Chapter 5

The next morning Smyth and his comrades awoke to find an overcast morning. They breakfasted and recapped on their proposed strategy for the benefit of Silas and Preston. Smyth split his men up into groups of two, except in the case of Tom and James. Tom would ride with Smyth and Duncannon, whilst James would accompany Silas and Caleb. Preston would be in charge of another man, leaving the remaining pair to carry out their part of the search together.

Smyth, Duncannon and Silas went to a concealed gunroom in a wing of the house only frequented by the most loyal staff. Every man was issued with a pistol, musket and powder and shot. They all had their own cutlasses as well. As they emerged from the house, they looked as though they were armed for going to a minor war.

Smyth saw the horses and realised he had never asked Tom or James if they could ride a horse. He called the two lads to him. 'Can either of you ride?'

Tom seemed reluctant to answer, and then said, 'I rode an old mare belonging to my dad's friend once.'

'As long as you can stay in the saddle you'll soon get used to it. What about you, James?'

'Yes sir, my father worked on a farm and taught me.'

'Good,' responded Smyth.

The small troop mounted their steeds and headed out of the stable yard and across the meadow to join the highway. About four miles along the road was the turn-off for Exeter. Smyth halted the small mounted band. 'Silas, this is where you turn off. Remember, if you discover anything really important send Caleb or James to fetch us.' He raised his voice so that everyone could hear him. 'The base to contact will be my friend at Northcott Manor.'

Smyth peeled his groups off at each of the road junctions until he, James Duncannon and Tom were left heading towards Plymouth.

On the route all the men had instructions to enquire if anyone had seen any furtive-looking strangers passing through their village in the last few days. They didn't have too far to go to find what they were looking for. In the hamlet of Pericote, Silas asked the local innkeeper if he had seen any strangers.

'Aye, three days ago four rough-looking characters with an old white-haired man rode into the village. Tale has it that they are living in an old disused barn to the north. It's about two miles from here.'

Caleb said he would take a ride up there and scout out the place. Silas meanwhile would send James some ten miles west to fetch his other colleagues to Pericote.

Two hours later Caleb was back. 'I found the place all right, Silas. Scrub and overgrown trees surround it. Some people are definitely living there. There is smoke rising out from the roof, so they have a cooking fire going.'

'We'll wait till the others arrive, then we'll make a raid on the barn,' said Silas.

Later that afternoon James and four of the men rode up to the little village inn. Silas was surprised to see four; he had only expected two men.

'It was lucky that James saw John and Samuel riding along an old coach road, so he asked them to come too,' said Henry, one of Smyth's staff on the mission.

Silas looked very pleased. 'That was sharp thinking of you, James. Can you use a pistol?'

'I have fired one, but never in anger.'

'Take my small spare pistol. Only use it if you have to.'

The seven riders made their way up to the barn. A hundred yards from the spot they dismounted and tied up the horses in the dense wood copse.

'There is a doorway at both ends of the building,' said Caleb.

'Right, two at one end, two at the other. Henry and me will go in through those windows, and James, you stay with the horses.' James felt a bit left out, but he wouldn't disobey Silas.

The doors burst open at each end and Silas and Henry jumped in through the window openings. Four men were seated round a small fire in the middle of the barn. A cooking pot was simmering over the fire. The startled men jumped to their feet and whirled round, trying their best to evaluate the situation.

A cutlass flashed from the belt of one of the brigands. Silas had his pistol cocked and ready to fire. He hit the man in the middle of his chest. Another levelled his pistol at one of Silas's men, about to fire. Caleb's cutlass hit him at the shoulder and very nearly decapitated him. The remaining two men saw the situation as hopeless and threw their hands in the air. Silas and Caleb disarmed them.

Caleb saw Johnson bundled up in a corner of the barn. He dashed over to him and cut the ropes binding him. 'Are you all right, Johnson?'

Johnson smiled and said, 'I am very glad to see

you, Caleb. Other than cramp in my old bones from being tied up, I am all right.'

Caleb helped him to his feet and assisted him to walk across to Silas and the others.

Silas's men found ropes and securely bound the two men. Silas hovered over the two men, brandishing his pistol menacingly. 'Now, I want some questions answered. If I don't get some answers, you will be digging pistol balls out of your bodies.' The two men grimaced in fear. 'Who are you working for?'

'A man called Donald Fortyscue. He paid us to kidnap the old man and told us to keep him until he called to fetch him,' replied one of the two, afraid that any hesitation would result in Silas using his pistol on him.

'Do you know where Fortyscue is and when he is calling to fetch Johnson?'

'No, sir, honestly we don't know any more than we have told you.'

The other man said, 'I heard that Fortyscue had turned to highway robbery to get money together. A constable from Exeter told a friend of mine that he was a wanted man.'

'So why did you work for him?' asked Silas.

'Money, sir. We all need money.'

Silas conferred with Caleb. 'I can't see any point in carting these two about with us. I'm thinking we should let them go free. They have no more to tell us.' Silas went back over to the two men. 'If you promise not to contact Fortyscue and return straight home, we will free you. You will bury your comrades' bodies first, though.' The men readily agreed.

Chapter 6

Silas and his comrades harnessed up the small pony trap to one of the horses that were grazing round the back of the barn. 'I presume you were brought here in this cart?' Silas asked.

Johnson replied, 'Yes I was, but I hope I can continue my travels with a little more comfort than when I came here. I was tied up and bundled in the cart.' The group laughed.

'So what are we to do now, Silas?' asked Caleb.

'I reckon that it will be unlikely that Fortyscue will be hiding in a small village. My guess is that he is hiding out in a large township. More places to get lost in. I say we all stay together and make our way to Northcott Manor. We can then establish contact with Captain Smyth.'

Meanwhile Smyth, Duncannon and Tom had been asking round all the dubious inns and hostelries in the Plymouth area. The three of them sat down to a simple meal of bread and cheese at an inn. 'I feel I have made a bit of a mess of this search, James. I have men spread out over most of the county, and we have no means of keeping in touch with each other. We don't know where Silas or any of the other men are.'

James Duncannon tried his best to placate his friend.

'Jonathan, you have done the best job with the resources you have. I suggest we go back to Northcott and await whatever news comes.' Smyth nodded with sadness.

The following afternoon Silas and his little party rumbled up the long driveway of Northcott Manor. One of the squire's servants looked out of the front windows and saw the little band approaching. 'Sir, sir, a group of men are approaching.'

Smyth heard the cry and jumped to his feet. He heard his friend, Squire Henry Felsham, hurrying across the wooden hall floor. Jonathan joined him at the large front door. A big grin broke over his face as he witnessed Silas and Caleb leading the little group up the drive.

He went out onto the drive and held his arms in a kind of praise to the heavens. 'Silas, Caleb, it is so good to see you.' He stopped as his eyes caught sight of Johnson with James Purdy in the cart. He helped Johnson out of the cart and flung his arms round him. 'Johnson, my old trusted friend. Are you all right? Where did they find you?'

'I am fine now, sir, thanks to your men. Some refreshment would be welcome, and Silas and Caleb will relate the story to you.'

The squire urged his cook to prepare food and drink for the newcomers to his manor. Meanwhile Smyth introduced them all to Henry Felsham, and Duncannon to Johnson. 'It is a great pleasure to meet you at last. I have heard so much about you,' said Duncannon as he shook hands with Johnson.

'Thank you. It is a pleasure to meet you too.'

At the dining table Silas brought his master up to

date with all the events they had experienced. When he had finished and Silas had told him his theory that their enemy might be hiding in a large town, Smyth banged his fist on the oak dining table. 'By thunder, Silas, you could be right. That hadn't crossed my mind. The question is, which big town? We have searched all round Plymouth with little sign of him.'

Silas suddenly remembered that one of the kidnappers had told him of the Exeter constable stating that a wanted poster existed around Exeter. When he related this news, Smyth took on a thoughtful look. 'It may be best if we travel to Exeter. We may find someone who knows where the man can be hiding.'

It was a short journey into Exeter from Northcott Manor, so little time was lost. The group split up: Smyth took Tom and Caleb, while Duncannon took James and two more of the party. Silas had the remaining men. Between them they scoured all the hostelries, inns and meeting places located in the town.

The sun was beginning to set as the little group converged at the agreed meeting place near the Cathedral Green.

'Has anybody discovered anything?' asked Smyth.

It was Caleb who answered. 'Aye, sir, it be only hearsay, but one of the locals was a-telling me that he heard some men sat in the Queens Head the other evening. They were talking about some highway robber fellow who'd been causing folk some grief round these parts. They reckon as he was heading towards Poole Harbour. Someone had seen him riding that way. They said the constables were a-chasing him, but he gave them the slip.'

Smyth thanked Caleb. The rest of the group had heard of the incidents of various robberies, but no one had a specific sighting. Smyth sat in silent thought for some time.

Duncannon interrupted his thoughts. 'Do you suppose he is planning to make for a ship in Poole?'

'That is the same thought that had crossed my mind, my friend. My thoughts were how to head him off. I was wondering if he is thinking of taking to the sea, we should consider conscripting the use of the *Pegasus*.'

Silas spoke up. 'Captain, I reckon that's a good idea. Even if he stays on land or gets aboard a ship, we would have him covered.'

Smyth nodded his acknowledgment of his old boatswain. 'Silas, take one of the boys with you and ride to Portsmouth and see if the *Pegasus* is still at harbour there. If she is, tell the crew what we would like them to do. I suggest you both sail with them to Poole and stand off shore there till we get there. We will borrow some signal flags and tell you what to do next. If she has gone, ride straight to Poole.'

Silas tipped a salute to his captain and beckoned to Tom. They headed outside to saddle up their horses and get on their way.

Smyth and Duncannon then made their arrangements with the rest of the little band. The plan was to make their way towards Poole. They would split up into groups and ask at all the villages and towns as they passed through as to any sightings of Fortyscue. Eventually they would meet up in the town centre of Poole.

It was four days later when Smyth next met up with

his men in the centre of Poole. 'Has anyone discovered any news?'

Duncannon spoke first. 'We stayed over in Dorchester for the night and asked at various taverns. A small band of robbers had been causing havoc around the area. I went to the local watch and discovered that they had given chase to this gang, but they lost them. They did say that they thought they were heading east.'

Caleb put his hand up to be noticed. 'Well, sir, we asked around as we passed through Stokeford, and struck gold, so to speak. Just four days earlier some of the locals spotted six men riding through the village. As they didn't cause any trouble, nobody bothered. They did say that the men were heavily armed.'

'Good work, men,' said Jonathan Smyth. He unrolled his linen map and spread it on the ground. Tracing his finger along the route of the sightings, he smiled and said, 'Well, it seems our guess was correct, they were headed this way. We'll head for the harbour and see what we can find out.'

At the harbour the group dismounted and tethered their horses. 'Meet here in one hour. Ask around at all the ships and boats.'

Just over half an hour later a shrill whistle pierced the air. Smyth stared round to see where the noise was coming from. 'Over there,' shouted young James. 'Caleb is beckoning you over.'

Smyth and Duncannon hurried over to Caleb on the other side of the harbour. 'What have you found, Caleb?'

Excitedly, Caleb spluttered out his news. 'Captain,

53

Donald Fortyscue and his men boarded a ship under cover of darkness two days ago and sailed out to sea.'

'How did you find that out, Caleb?'

'Step aboard that ship there and ask the captain. He saw the whole thing.'

Smyth strode over to the vessel and asked permission to go aboard. 'Sir, one of my men tells me you may have some news for me.'

The captain looked Jonathan Smyth up and down and recognised that he was about to address a man of quality. Even though Smyth had been journeying for some days, he still looked very smart in his dark red velvet jacket and ruffled collared shirt and cravat. His knee-length riding boots needed polishing, but that only proved he had journeyed a long distance. 'How can I help you, sir?' asked the captain.

'My man says you saw a group of men set out to sea two days past. Do you know what ship they sailed on?'

The old captain stroked his grey beard and studied Smyth's face before answering. 'Can I ask what your interest in these men is?'

'Sir, all these men are wanted by the law. They are highway robbers and they have done my family a great harm. I have been granted permission from the King himself to bring these men to justice.'

The old man whistled through his teeth at the statement. 'They looked well-armed, but I never thought that they were wanted men. A few days ago a ship came in and anchored offshore. Their shore boat came into the harbour and tied up. They bought some supplies, and two of the crew met the leader of the band of men you are chasing. I decided that something was odd about this ship – why didn't they tie up in the harbour? I fetched my telescope from my cabin and decided to take a spy at the ship standing off shore. Blow me, it had twelve guns on the side facing me. You have to wonder why a ship with twenty-four cannon should sail into Poole Harbour. The last thing this place is is a naval base. Me and my men decided to keep an eye on the comings and goings of the crew. Some time later these robbers, as you call them, were rowed out to the ship. That night at high tide I watched the ship sail out to sea.'

'I don't suppose you saw the name of the ship?' asked Smyth.

'I sent one of my men to look to see if the shore boat bore the ship's name. It did. The name was the *Wild Rover.*'

Chapter 7

Jonathan Smyth was jubilant. All the searching, travelling and the many, many questions that the group had had to ask of people at all the towns and villages over the last few weeks seemed now to have paid dividends. He turned to Duncannon and said, 'I can tell you why that ship would not enter Poole Harbour, or any other harbour for that matter. The *Wild Rover* has a notorious reputation for being a pirate ship. What I fail to understand is why somebody like Fortyscue would wish to join up with somebody like the captain of that vessel. His name is Daniel Bland. People who know of him have nicknamed him Deadly Dan. He has no compulsion about slitting anyone's throat. It makes me wonder if my former friend has any idea of this man's reputation.'

Duncannon didn't hesitate. 'I suppose this pirate and his crew have a bounty on their heads?'

'By most of the seafaring nations in Europe, I would think. What is your point, James?'

'Well, that being the case, if he, his crew and ship were captured and brought to justice, a large reward would be forthcoming.'

'I would think a reward would be gladly paid if someone was brave enough to carry it off. Bland and his crew are one of the most ruthless and ferocious bands of renegades to sail the seven seas. Many a ship and its crew lie on the seabed because of being unfortunate enough to have stumbled into the path of the *Wild Rover* and Daniel Bland.'

'Surely with our combined expertise of seafaring and battle experience, we should better this man,' replied Duncannon.

'I fear without Silas turning up with the *Pegasus*, we have no hope,' responded Smyth.

The following morning Smyth and Duncannon were seated having breakfast at the inn they were lodging at. They heard a pair of heavy shoes running across the stone flagged floor. 'Captain, Captain, the *Pegasus* is here.' It was Samuel, one of Smyth's men.

'Steady up, man. Catch your breath and tell me what news you have.'

Samuel sat down beside his captain, breathed deeply and began again. 'Caleb asked me to go down to the harbour early this morning. I saw a four-master standing about a half mile out at sea. I then went to see that ship's master you were a-talking to yesterday and asked to borrow his telescope. Blow me, it was the *Pegasus* I spied. I thanked the captain and ran to the harbour point, took off my shirt and waved it as hard as I could.'

'Good man, Samuel. I shall borrow some signal flags and send them a message to come into the harbour.'

'There's no need, sir. They spied me waving and I watched them lower the shore boat. They are coming ashore.'

'Excellent, Samuel. Thank you. Get the rest of the men ready and we will be down on the harbour directly.'

Fifteen minutes later Smyth and his small band of

men were hugging and shaking hands with their old shipmates who they hadn't seen for weeks. 'It's really good to see you again, Captain, and you, Captain Duncannon. Silas told us what has happened, and we are only too willing to help any way we can.'

Smyth and Duncannon thanked them profusely. 'I suggest we all sail out to the *Pegasus* and discuss the next step.'

On board the *Pegasus* Smyth settled himself in his old cabin. Nothing seemed to have changed since he was last on board as the vessel's master. James Duncannon sat beside him with charts set out before them. 'Would you mind sending for Silas?' asked Smyth.

Duncannon stood up and went to open the door. Silas was about to knock on the captain's cabin door. 'I was just about to send for you, Silas.' Both men smiled at the coincidence and Silas entered the cabin. 'Are we provisioned for what may turn out to be a lengthy sea voyage?'

'Aye, aye, sir. I used that purse of silver you gave me to stock the ship with provisions. I also checked on the stock of gunpowder and shot. The magazine is full as we left it.'

'Good man, Silas. Now, down to business. Who has been in charge of the ship since we left her?'

Silas stroked his stubbly chin. 'Apparently Clem Oates was voted in by the men as ship's master, but as they never left the dockside he hasn't been put to the test.'

Smyth glanced at Duncannon. 'Good choice as master. He has good common sense and he is intelligent. We had better ask him if he minds us taking over for a while. Can you fetch him?'

Minutes later, Clem Oates followed Silas into the cabin. Smyth asked him if he would mind if he re-assumed captaincy until this matter with the fugitives had been settled. 'Captain, I wouldn't pretend to step into your role while you were here. The men only voted me as captain while you were absent. Nobody has slept in your cabin while you were away. I wouldn't let them. Me and the crew always knew you would be back, so we kept everything the way you insisted.'

'Well, thank you, Clem. I propose that you and Silas share the duties of boatswain and split the duties so you don't conflict with each other's orders.' Both men gave their captain the curled-fingered salute, then shook hands and left the cabin to prepare the ship for sea.

Smyth and Duncannon sat for some time looking over the charts on the table and discussing where their enemies might be heading. After a while in thoughtful silence Duncannon looked at his friend and said, 'If I were a man with such a bounty on my head, I think there could be very few places that I would be able to go.'

Smyth interrupted his friend with a grin on his face, 'And where would that place be, James?'

'The West Indies, my friend.'

Jonathan banged his fist down on the table in jubilation. 'Excellent, my thoughts entirely. That is where we should make sail for without further delay.' He jumped up from his chair; made for the door and shouted, 'Full sail. We head for the Caribbean.'

Chapter 8

Tom and James soon found out that life aboard a sailing ship wasn't easy. It was their first day out to sea, and the weather was good. The *Pegasus* was under full sail and was cutting through the sea easily. Tom broke off from his task of helping to scrub the decks. He straightened his back to look out to sea. The ship was bowing gently into the waves. The sails were billowing full of wind, and looking over the side, he realised that they seemed to be cutting through the waves at a good speed. 'This is a marvellous life,' he remarked to James.

His friend grinned at him. 'It'll be better when we've finished this job.'

Silas was watching them from the poop deck with a grin on his face. Captain Smyth walked up silently behind him. 'Making the lads earn their keep, Silas?'

'Aye, sir, gets the young'uns used to the idea that they aren't paying guests.' Smyth gave Silas a friendly tap on the shoulder and went on with his inspection. Most of the other seamen were going about the tasks set for them and acknowledged their captain as he passed them.

That evening after the two lads had eaten they went to sit on the deck. Both boys were really tired and sat together in silence. Later in their bunks sleep came to them easily. Tom and James awoke the next morning to feel the ship pitching from side to side. They dressed quickly and went on deck. The sky was dark and grey. A heavy wind was blowing up from the south-west. The force of the wind seemed to be making the sea boil beneath them. Tom looked up into the rigging. About half of the sails had been rolled up and slung to the yards. Tom looked at his friend. 'Jamie, do you feel all right?'

'No, I feel sick. I must go below.'

On their way below they saw Silas. 'James is feeling sick. Can he go back to his bunk?'

Silas grinned. 'Aye, he may get used to it in time. Are you all right, Tom?'

'I am at the moment, but that could change.'

'Stay below, both of you.'

All that day the ship pitched and tossed its way across the unforgiving sea. Two hours after James becoming sick, Tom felt the onset of seasickness and crawled into his bunk. The third day saw a brighter sky and the sea a little less ferocious. Both Tom and James awoke feeling hungry. They dressed and went to join the rest of the crew eating breakfast. 'Feeling better, lads?' was the greeting from some of the crewmen. Tom and James gave a sheepish acknowledgment that they had survived their first experience of seasickness.

It seemed to be another fifteen or sixteen days that had passed, but Tom and James weren't really sure. Days and nights appeared to blend from one day to the next and they weren't keeping count of their days aboard ship. Some days were stormy, some misty, but now they seemed to have reached a part of the world

61

where it was warm and sunny most days. Tom decided that he would be bold enough to ask Captain Smyth of their whereabouts. He was making his daily inspection when Tom approached him.

'Morning, Captain. May I ask you where we are and when we expect to see land?'

Smyth smiled, 'It's been a long journey for your first voyage, Tom. We have entered the waters of the Caribbean. We expect to see land any time this day.'

'Where is the Caribbean?'

'Have you ever heard of the Americas?'

'Yes, sir, I remember seeing a map of the world and noticing the big block of land known as the Americas.'

'Well, we are in the sea approaching the middle of that block of land. There are many islands in this part of the sea, and we have to find where our enemy may have docked his ship. It will not be easy, but we think we have a good idea where they are.'

'Thank you, sir.'

Smyth carried on with his inspection and strode away as though he was walking down a village street.

Silas decided that he would teach the boys the art of knot tying to keep their minds busy. The long warm day began its gradual journey into night. The sun's golden yellow glow began to change colour to a redder gold as it started to set beyond the horizon.

'Land ho,' was the cry from high in the main mast. Silas was the first on deck, followed by Smyth, Duncannon and Clem. The sailor in the crow's nest was frantically pointing to where he had seen land. Telescopes were put to the officers' eyes scouring the horizon. It was Duncannon who broke the silence created by eager observation. 'Bahamas, I think?'

Smyth lowered his telescope and said, 'You could

be right, James. Let's go and consult our charts. Silas.'
The three of them went below to mull over the charts.
Minutes later they decided that what they had seen
was indeed the main island of the Bahamas group
of islands. Smyth's face took on a puzzled look.
'What's on your mind, Jonathan?'

'It would be wise to dock at Nassau and ask a few
questions, but I wager they have gone to Jamaica.
More chance of integrating into the miscreants that
make their base there.'

The *Pegasus* tied up into the dock in Nassau in the
dawn of the next day. Silas and Clem had been in
discussion with Smyth and Duncannon and went on
deck to issue their orders. 'Fifteen men to stay aboard
and look after the ship. The remainder to go ashore
and ask the local people if they have seen any new
shipping, especially the *Wild Rover*. Caleb will take
five men with him and buy fresh supplies.' Silas
finished his orders with the time that everyone must
be back aboard.

It was early evening when the crew reassembled on
the main deck, ready to sail on the high tide. Smyth,
Duncannon and Silas stood on the poop and addressed
the muster of men on the main deck. 'Has anyone
found any news of interest?' Two hands were raised.
'Well?' asked Silas.

One of the men spoke. 'We were a-talking to some
sailors in one of the inns in the town.'

A laugh went up from some of the crew. 'Might
have known they would be a-drinking,' cried one of
the men.

'Anyhow,' resumed the first man scowling, 'these sailors saw a three-master dock here no more'an three days since. Said they took on supplies and left next day.'

'Did they see the name of the ship?' asked Smyth.

'None of 'em could read, but one of 'em knew the word *Rover*.'

Smyth looked delighted. 'By Jove, it's them. Weigh anchor and full sail, Silas. We sail due south for Jamaica.'

With all the sails full of the evening wind, the *Pegasus* ploughed through the darkening seas on its journey south towards the island of Jamaica. In the afternoon of the following day they were in view of land again. Smyth saw Tom and James looking out to sea. 'The land you see over there is Cuba. We are about to sail through a strip of ocean called the Windward Passage and then on to Jamaica.'

The lads had been overawed with events so far, and now was no exception. When he had left them, James said, 'These are places you only see on maps. I never thought I would see them.'

'Me neither,' replied his friend.

Smyth and Duncannon held a meeting with Silas and Clem in the captain's cabin. 'Our guess is that the *Wild Rover* is headed for Port Royal, Kingston. If what the men found out is true, they have two days' start on us. With this wind we may catch some of that time up, as we have more masts and more sails. I am hoping that we catch them before they reach Kingston.' Duncannon and the two boatswains couldn't find an argument against their master's reasoning.

Duncannon suggested that Clem and Silas check that all their armaments and men were in instant readiness for when they made contact with the *Wild Rover*. Smyth agreed. They went on to lay out the line of command and strategy: Smyth would take overall command and take control of manoeuvring the ship into position; Duncannon would take full control of the cannons along with Clem. Any boarding party would be left up to Silas.

They were now back into open seas, as they had sailed through the Windward Passage. The wind was still in their favour, and the *Pegasus* was cutting through the waves like an expert skater on ice.

Two days later the *Pegasus* was nearing Jamaica. In the far distance they could see the landmass that they were heading towards. The crewman who had the job of watching from the crow's nest shrieked out the words everyone was waiting to hear.

Chapter 9

'Ship ahoy. Larboard side.' Telescopes were produced. 'Too far away yet,' proclaimed Duncannon. 'All we can say is, it is a ship.'

'A three-master,' corrected Smyth.

Two hours later the officers were looking out anxiously to sea, using their telescopes. They had gained on the three-mast vessel, and Smyth estimated that they were some five miles away from land, with the other ship about a mile further away from them nearer the island of Jamaica. 'We are still on the west coast of the island, so she has still some way to go to reach Port Royal. If that is the *Rover*, it will be better if we can capture her out at sea rather than near a port.'

Minutes later Duncannon's eye and telescope confirmed that it was the *Wild Rover*. 'Fetch Clem,' called Jonathan Smyth. 'Clem, can you find us a distress flag in the store?'

Clem looked puzzled at the request, but didn't question it. Some minutes later he arrived back on deck with the appropriate flags.

'Get somebody to hoist them quickly.'

'What's your plan, Jonathan?' asked Duncannon.

'I am hoping that if they see a distress signal hoisted they will think we are an easy target for boarding and will want to approach to capture us.'

'That's very devious of you, Jonathan.'

'You know what they say about the like minds of thieves.'

Duncannon laughed, 'I hardly consider you a thief, but you have been forced into a shady past.'

The pirate captain requested a telescope. He wanted to obtain a closer look at the approaching ship. 'The ship has no country flag but she is signalling that she is in distress,' said Daniel Bland.

His right-hand man grinned. 'She may be crippled, and she could be carrying gold.'

Bland looked at his mate, and a broad grin crept across his bearded face. 'My thoughts as well, matey.'

Fortyscue came up to Bland. 'What's the problem?'

'A ship in distress. She'll be in even more distress when we've boarded her. Get your men ready and armed. With luck we'll have another ship by the end of the day.'

Smyth took off his coat and put on a rough seaman's jacket he had borrowed from one of the crew.

'What are you doing?' asked Duncannon.

'Trying to look in need of help. I suggest you do the same if you are going to stand on the deck where our enemy will see you. If they see you in officer's clothes they may smell a rat.'

'I'll borrow a jacket immediately.' With that Duncannon dashed out of the cabin. Minutes later Smyth was standing on the deck looking shabby and somewhat helpless.

* * *

Bland put his telescope to his eye to view the ship they were approaching. He saw Smyth and Duncannon standing, waving to them. 'By Black Jake's beard, they look a motley rabble. This should be an easy task.' His crew laughed out loud, especially with the thought of looting through another ship's belongings and hopefully a bit of gold and valuables to share between them.

'Steady as she goes, Silas. As soon as the *Rover* gets within two hundred yards of us, pull to her stern and steer around the back of her. James, when I give the order, let off a fusillade of cannon into the stern. Attempt to destroy her steering.' Duncannon nodded his approval and quickly made his way to the gun deck.

The *Wild Rover* edged ever closer. Bland reviewed the situation through his telescope. If there were the slightest sign of trouble, he would order his men to open fire on the *Pegasus*. Smyth was still waving plaintively at the *Rover* and the *Pegasus*'s cannon doors were still shut, so no need to worry, thought Bland.

'Now, Silas, bring us round to their stern.' With the sudden rudder movement, the *Pegasus* leaned over.
Bland had his first concerns that something was wrong. 'What are they doing?' he asked his mate. It was a worry too late for Daniel Bland. Within minutes the *Pegasus* was moving rapidly towards the stern of the *Wild Rover* and a broadside from Bland's ship wouldn't achieve anything. The cannon doors on the

Pegasus opened rapidly and twenty-four cannons protruded from the ports. '*Fire!*' An earth-rending series of explosions were detonated. Some of the cannonballs missed their target and fell harmlessly into the sea. The problem for Daniel Bland was that more than half of the cannonade had destroyed the stern of his ship.

Duncannon had the gun crew reload as rapidly as they could. '*Fire!*' A second fusillade of cannonballs sunk their way into the shattered stern of the *Rover*, this second volley proving fatal for the ship. Duncannon's gun crew had succeeded in hitting the vessel below the water line. The *Wild Rover* began a slow descent into the sea.

Bland was not to be overcome so easily. After the first cannonade hit his ship, he realised he had been outwitted. His object was now to pull as close as possible to the *Pegasus* so his men could board her. He now needed the *Pegasus* more than ever.

'Stand by to repel boarders,' was Smyth's command to his crew. Cannons were now useless at such close quarters. Smyth's crew rushed onto the deck, armed to the teeth. Bland's men were throwing grappling hooks towards the *Pegasus*. As one landed the *Pegasus*'s crew were feverishly cutting the ropes, but that didn't stop some of the pirates managing to pull themselves on board. The pirates' primary thought was that of survival. Their ship was sinking.

Smyth's men were now engaged in a hand-to-hand battle on the main deck. Tom and James picked up a spare sword each and decided that fighting for their lives was better than suffering a dreadful fate if the pirates won the day. Cries of extreme pain from seamen being slashed and cut by flailing cutlasses mingled with the clash of steel on steel. Smyth and

Duncannon were standing back to back, taking on all comers, as were Silas and Clem. Their blades were flashing from one opponent to another.

Two of the pirates had got themselves a small vantage point. They had climbed partway up the main mast with the intention of shooting Captain Smyth. They had considered that they would be able to shoot their pistols down on either Smyth or Duncannon.

Tom happened to glance up at the mast. 'Jamie, look up there, two men going to shoot into the crowd.'

'At the Captain, most likely,' said James.

They scanned the deck quickly. Weapons were now lying everywhere from combatants who were dead or injured. James picked up three pistols and Tom retrieved a further long-barrelled pistol. 'I've never fired a pistol before.'

'Just aim and pull the trigger.'

James took as careful aim as he could and pulled the trigger. The explosion temporarily deafened him. A howl of pain emitted from one of the men hanging on the mast. James had hit him in the leg.

The other pirate looked to where the shooting was coming from and levelled his pistol at the boys. He was too late: Silas had spotted the man and aimed at him and hit him in the head. The man fell like a stone onto the deck. Tom aimed his pistol at the wounded man, still hanging from the mast, and fired. The shot hit the man squarely in the chest. He too dropped to the deck, dead.

Bland saw his opportunity and leapt at Smyth. Duncannon pushed Smyth to one side and raised his cutlass as Bland leapt. The downward swing of his blade cut across Daniel Bland's shoulder. Blood erupted from the wound. He dropped his sword.

Duncannon wasn't in the mood for taking prisoners. He thrust the cutlass straight into the pirate captain's ribcage. This encounter was Daniel Bland's last one on earth.

The crew of the *Rover* were now beaten. Any left standing gave themselves up to their victors. Smyth quickly scanned the faces of the vanquished men as they were being clapped in chains to go below decks. It only took him seconds to see Donald Fortyscue among the pirates. He now had a thick beard and his dark hair was thick and straggly, but Smyth recognised him. 'You, my friend,' he said sarcastically, 'you will not suffer the cells of a Jamaican prison. You will feel the hangman's noose back in England.'

A rollcall revealed that Smyth had lost six of his men in the battle. That night aboard the ship a sombre attitude was prevalent among the crew at the loss of their shipmates.

The *Pegasus* docked at Port Royal in Jamaica and the prisoners were led off the ship in chains to face the military prison pending their subsequent trial for piracy. Jonathan Smyth and James Duncannon sought an audience with the island's ruling Governor. The following day their request was granted. Duncannon introduced himself as a serving Post Captain in his Majesty's Royal Navy. He told the Governor the series of events that ended in a battle off Jamaica, and of his friend Jonathan Smyth's plight and of his long fight to return his enemy to England to face justice.

After listening to the whole saga, the Governor ordered his clerk to produce an official letter for Smyth to take back with him to England. 'Deliver this to the Lord Chief Justice in London. This letter will ensure that the reward for the capture of Daniel Bland and his pirates is afforded to you and your crew. You have done us all a great service in ridding us of these pirates.' On the following day's tide the *Pegasus* started the return journey to England.

Whilst Silas was on watch one evening, Jonathan Smyth came out onto the deck and decided to chat with his old friend.

'I've been meaning to tell you, Captain. You owe a debt of gratitude to those two boys. If it hadn't been for them, both you and Captain Duncannon might not have been here.'

Smyth asked why. Silas told him about the incident of the pirates climbing the mast to shoot them. Smyth stroked his fair hair back and smiled. 'I had no idea, Silas. Thank you for telling me. The lads won't go unrewarded.'

The following day Jonathan made a special effort to thank the two lads. 'When we get back home, I would deem it a great honour if both of you would stay on the estate with me. If you accept my offer, I will visit your parents and put the proposal to them. You will have access to horses to enable you to visit your mothers and fathers anytime you please. I will ensure that you are coached in estate management so that one day you will be able to run the estate on your own terms. As you are aware, I have no family left now, and when I am gone someone else will take over the ownership. It will be better if it is someone I feel deserves it.'

Tom and James stared at each other, not believing the proposition they had been offered.

'Don't give your answer now. Think it over. We have at least two weeks till we dock in England.'

Later, Smyth and Duncannon decided to question Donald Fortyscue. 'How did you know I was being pardoned and intended returning to Credlington Manor? Every step of our journey, you appeared to be one jump ahead of us. You have nothing to gain or lose by telling us your secret.'

Fortyscue sniggered, 'I guessed that bit would rattle you. I think I may take my secret to my grave and leave you to ponder it forever.'

'Oh, I will not worry my head about you once you are hanged,' replied Smyth, who was relying on Donald Fortyscue's arrogance. It didn't fail him.

'I was always better than you, Smyth, even as children I was smarter than you.'

Jonathan shrugged his shoulders. The man's arrogance was surfacing quicker than ever now. He was demonstrating that whilst he was in irons he was still better than his one-time friend. 'I knew someone in the Admiralty who introduced me to a senior officer of his. I met this man socially and paid him to keep me abreast of any movements being made in regard to you. When I received information I acted. You see, you wouldn't have had the brains to do that, Jonathan, would you?'

'No, but when we are talking about being smart I am not in chains.' With that Jonathan stood up, followed by Duncannon, and they ascended the ladder to the main deck.

Chapter 10

During the course of the long voyage home, James Duncannon had been troubled about Fortyscue's comment that he had obtained his information from someone in the Admiralty. His discussion with Smyth about it was that he had to find out who the traitor was. After all if he was handing out that information for money, what else was the person selling?

Meanwhile Tom and James had been discussing the pros and cons of accepting Jonathan Smyth's generous offer. The pros were definitely greater than the cons, but how would their parents accept the news?

Almost three weeks later the *Pegasus* pulled alongside the dock in England. Tom and James asked Smyth if they could go home and talk to their parents before finally giving him their answer. James Duncannon told Smyth that he must go with all speed to the Admiralty and get his superiors to root out the person who had sold the information. Smyth once again said his farewells to his ship's crew. He had promised them that he would seek and collect the reward for the capture of the pirate crew of the *Wild Rover*. When next he contacted them, it would be to share the reward out between the crew. Nearly everyone was sad to see the group splitting up like this, but they all knew it must be so.

Smyth, Silas and Caleb set out to collect Johnson, who had been recovering from his ordeal at Northcott Manor with Henry Felsham. Tom and James had been provided with two horses to carry them back home to Kingsport.

Tom told his mother and father of his adventure on the *Pegasus* and of the proposal offered by Jonathan Smyth. He had no doubt that James was doing the same. 'I thought you were going back to the boatyard to see if you could get your old job back,' said his father.

Tom looked downcast. 'The job at the boatyard would be always doing the same thing day after day, year after year. With Captain Smyth's offer, James and I could be running a whole private estate in time. I can make something of my life.'

'You like this Jonathan Smyth, don't you? Do you trust him?' asked his mother.

Tom noticed she had moisture in her eyes. 'Yes, I like him very much, and I have already trusted him with my life. But I love you very much and I can see you regularly. It is only twenty or thirty miles away on horseback.'

'We only want what is best for you,' Tom's father said at last. 'Go and follow your instincts and hopefully your fortune.' Tom's mother hugged her son.

'Smyth has promised he will meet you and talk to you,' said Tom.

Tom met James in the High Street as they had arranged. 'Will they let you go?' Tom asked his friend.

'At first they said no. Then they said they would make their decision after meeting Captain Smyth. How have you fared?'

'They said that I should follow my instincts, but they also want to meet Captain Smyth.'

The following day the two boys saddled their horses and set out for Credlington Manor. Jonathan Smyth was delighted to see them once more. The boys told him of their conversations with their parents. 'Tomorrow you can set off back to your homes and invite them here to look round the house and estates, which will be your new home if they agree.'

Silas had the coach teamed up to four large horses and Tom and James accompanied him back to their parents' houses. Tom's mother was all in a fluster; she said she had nothing fine enough to wear.

'I have been given money to pay for a new calico dress for you, Mum. Captain Smyth has given James the same for his mother.'

With the mothers in new dresses and the fathers wearing the best they had, the coach with the parents and the two boys riding alongside made their way back to Credlington Manor. Smyth was on the huge main doorway to meet his guests. He looked resplendent in a scarlet three-quarter-length coat, white frilly cravat, black knee breeches and shiny knee-length boots. A lavish meal was laid on and a tour round the gardens afterwards. Tom's mother was holding her son's arm whilst walking round the grounds. 'Isn't he a handsome man?'

'Mother!'

After the walk Jonathan talked to all the parents about his ideas for the boys' future, whilst Tom and James watched Silas and Caleb busying themselves in the stable yard.

The parents met up with their boys later. Tom's dad had only one sentence to say: 'Tom, you'd be foolish to reject this position.'

'Hear hear,' piped up James's father.

The two lads whooped for joy at the reactions.

They rushed into the big house and saw Jonathan Smyth in the drawing room. 'We're coming to live with you.' He hugged the boys.

Three weeks later a horse was heard trotting down the gravel driveway towards the manor house's front door. Tom went to the door to see who their visitor was. 'Captain Duncannon, how wonderful to see you.' Duncannon was resplendent in his full naval uniform, with a shiny sword scabbard hanging at his polished black belt. He had come with news.

Seated in the drawing room, Duncannon told Jonathan of the happenings at the Admiralty. 'A major enquiry was instigated to root out the man responsible for the leak of information. We discovered the man who met Fortyscue and introduced him to our mole. From then on it became a fairly simple task. Questioning that individual revealed the man. He was a Lieutenant Alfred Johnson, who was then held in custody and questioned repeatedly. He revealed he had serious gambling debts and needing the money to pay off his creditors. He had carried out the offence on two occasions, one being against you. The naval authorities are to imprison him and he has been dishonourably discharged from the service.'

'I have news for you too, my friend,' said Smyth. 'I have placed at my bank the reward money for bringing the pirates to justice. I intend that it will be shared equally between you and the crew of the *Pegasus* and Silas and Caleb.' Duncannon shook his friend's hand warmly as he thanked him.

'So that is the end of our adventure, James Duncannon.'

'Till the next time, Jonathan, old friend.'

Tom and James entered the room to catch the last of the conversation.

BOOK 2

Call to Arms

Chapter 1

It was a very chilly morning following a night of early hard frost in the beginning of November in the Year of Our Lord 1733. A large brown horse came galloping into the courtyard of Credlington Manor, its rider hurriedly dismounting. The horse's nostrils were flared from the long gallop, its breath showing up like steam on the morning chill. 'Get a blanket on this mare, will you? And get it into the stable,' the blond-haired man instructed the scurrying groom. Jonathan Smyth, the owner and baronet of Credlington Manor, strode purposely across the yard to the heavy oak front door.

He entered the large entrance hall to be greeted by Johnson his butler. He took off his heavy double-shouldered long riding coat and wide-brimmed hat and handed them to Johnson. 'Bring me some mulled wine into my study and see if anyone can run and find Silas, please.'

'Yes, sir. I will get one of the servants to run over to the big barns. I believe they are working there.'

Smyth opened the door to his study to be met by the welcoming heat from the glowing fire dancing in the hearth of the big stone fireplace. The study walls were lined in mellow oak panelling, with one large mullioned window looking out onto well-kept lawns edged with privet. Jonathan Smyth seated himself in a leather chair beside the warming fire, rubbing his hands as he warmed them in front of the glow.

Minutes later Johnson appeared with his master's mulled wine. 'I have sent one of the kitchen boys to fetch Silas. He should be with you soon, sir.'

Smyth thanked his butler and began to sip his warm drink. Some ten minutes later a sharp knock rattled the study door. 'Come in,' shouted Smyth.

A tall heavily-built man with dark, thinning hair entered the study. He wore a sailor's reefer jacket buttoned up to two buttons below his neck. His neck was adorned with a red linen scarf and his heavy-duty breeches were complemented with thick, dark grey knee-high stockings. 'Good morning, Silas.'

'Morning, Cap'n, you sent for me?'

'Yes, I have had some very disturbing news. I have been to visit one of my banks in Totnes and an acquaintance of mine stopped me in the street and told me that my old friend Squire Brassington had been burgled and part of his house badly burned.'

Silas took on a look of shock, even though he didn't know the man. 'What do you require from me then, sir?'

'Us, Silas. Get Caleb, Tom and James ready for riding over towards Kingsport, and leave Preston to look after the farm workers. Make sure you all have swords, pistols and warm clothing.'

Silas gave his usual curled-hand salute, his finger touching his temple, and quickly left the room.

A lot had happened in the six years since Tom and James had met Jonathan Smyth. After their adventure on the *Pegasus*, Smyth had given the two lads a permanent post on his estate. At the weekends they went home to visit both their parents. During the working week the lads worked under the direction of Silas. In the evenings Smyth had them taught by a private tutor for three years. Silas had also been involved in teaching the lads. He had taught them how to use pistols, blunderbusses and sword fighting. They were equipped for fending off any enemy.

Half an hour later Smyth walked out from his front door into the courtyard. He was again clothed in his broad-brimmed hat, heavy riding coat and shiny black riding boots. He smiled as he came face to face with Tom and James, now young men about six feet tall, broad-shouldered and handsome. Silas, Caleb, Tom and James were all dressed in heavy riding coats, long boots and hats. The broad black belts each had round their waists held a sword and two long-barrelled pistols. 'Morning Tom, James, Caleb. Are you all ready for a long ride?'

'Yes, sir,' responded Tom. 'Where are we going?'

'We ride to my friend's estate in a small hamlet near Kingsport. I will explain as we ride.'

The five riders and horses moved at a walking pace out of the courtyard and out onto the highway. As they trotted along Smyth told his companions of the news he had heard. 'I wish to see my old friend and discover if we can be of any assistance to him and his family.'

Chapter 2

It was nightfall when the five men arrived at Windfell Manor, Squire Brassington's home. They couldn't see much in the dark. What they did witness disturbed them. Silhouetted against the frosty night sky, the burnt skeleton-like structure of the west wing roof loomed ominously into the dark blue background of the sky. 'Good God. From what I can see part of the house is ruined.'

They dismounted and walked towards the part of the house, which had a light shining from its opened curtained windows. Smyth rapped loudly on the big front door. Moments later the door creaked open and a man stood in the dimly lit doorway, a blunderbuss cocked at the ready. Smyth quickly removed his hat so he could be recognised. 'Oh, Mr Smyth. I beg your pardon, sir. Forgive me, but everyone here is very scared since the raid.'

'That is understandable. Is your master available?'

'Yes, sir, come in and get warm.' The five of them gratefully accepted the invitation and moved into the hallway.

'My master is laid up in bed. If you go up the stairs, his room is the first on the right-hand side.'

Smyth handed his hat and coat to Silas and hurried up the broad hardwood stairway. He tapped lightly on the bedroom door and entered. The room was dimly lit with a glowing fire dancing in the fireplace.

This seemed to provide more illumination than the solitary candle.

'George, are you awake?'

A feeble voice responded. 'Who is it?'

'Jonathan Smyth. I only heard about your predicament this morning whilst I was in Totnes.'

'Oh, Jonathan. Thank you for coming. It must have been a long ride for you. Are you alone?'

'No, I have brought four of my men with me. We weren't sure what we would find when we got here.'

'Light that other candle and pull a chair over to the bed.'

As he did as he was instructed, Smyth looked on his friend George's face. The man's face was cut and bruised, and a large bandage was wrapped around his head with dried blood on its surface. George awkwardly pulled himself into a sitting position in the bed.

'My God,' exclaimed Jonathan, 'what have they done to you?'

'They beat me as I was trying to stop them. They murdered two of my workers and took just about anything of value from the house. Luckily I had no money in the house. It was only the day before that I put what money I had in the house into one of your banks. When they couldn't find anything of real value, they beat some of my servants and then set fire to the house. We put out the fire using buckets. We formed a human chain from the pond and managed to get the better of the fire, but not before it had devastated the west wing of the house.'

'Who did it?' asked a shocked Jonathan Smyth.

'We are not sure. All we know is that there were a lot of them, all heavily armed. I have heard that they have ransacked other properties in the area.'

'I will get to the bottom of this and see that you are avenged. If it is all right with you, I will get your servants to look after my men for the night, and tomorrow we will get down to an investigation.'

'Surely; that is the least I can offer you, my friend.'

The following morning Jonathan and his men awoke to another frosty but sunny day. They breakfasted in the manor house's large kitchen and afterwards dressed themselves for another ride.

Jonathan climbed the stairs to see the condition of his friend. 'I am feeling a little better this morning. I may get up later now that the headache and dizziness seem to have gone. Will you be back later?'

'We are going to find out what damage has been done and try to find out who did this. I think we should be back by nightfall.' With that Smyth turned on his heel and headed back down the main stairway and out into the courtyard.

Tom, James, Silas and Caleb were already outside, viewing the fire damage. The tiles had almost disappeared from the roof. The large rafters had burnt through at the ridge, leaving the bottom of the spars charred but still standing. The building resembled the skeleton of some prehistoric monster standing out against the sunlit sky. Inside the west wing they discovered that just about all the internal structure had been destroyed by the blaze. Just a fraction of the floor joists had been left balancing precariously from the holes that they sat in in the walls.

Silas approached Jonathan and said, 'Cap'n, if we find these brigands, we are only five against a lot of desperate men.'

'Don't worry, Silas, I don't think we shall be coming face to face with these people yet. I want to speak with the watchman today, to see what he is doing about all this.'

As the small band approached the hamlet they saw the full extent of the horror that had been wreaked upon the little community. People were wandering about with their belongings. Most of the cottages had been torched, and their thatched roofs had blazed like tinder. The fires had been so intense that the walls of many of the buildings had collapsed. 'Spread out and ask these people what they know about their invaders,' ordered Smyth.

Over an hour later Jonathan's men gathered together to talk over what they had found out. Caleb was the first to speak. 'One family told me they ran into the woods to escape being killed. The man in the family said he thought there were about twenty to twenty-five men, all heavily armed. He thought they might have been sailors, but not naval men wearing uniforms. They were roughly dressed and wearing handkerchiefs and tricorn hats.'

Tom butted in, 'One family told me basically the same story. They noticed that some of the men had large tattoos on their arms.'

'One man I spoke to said they may have had a ship that had sailed up the river towards Kingsport,' said Silas.

Smyth reflected on what had been said. Tom, who had by now become used to his moods and expressions, knew that he was deep in thought and possibly not listening to anymore of the ongoing conversation. His men continued to chatter about the things they had witnessed, voicing opinions of what steps should be done. Smyth jumped up from the tree log he had used as his resting place. 'Stay here. I am off to talk to the watch. Tom, you ride with me.' With that they mounted their grazing horses, pulled on the reins to bring the animals back to action and galloped away from the little band.

Ten miles further north was the market town for the area. Smyth and Tom ushered their steeds at a trot down the main thoroughfare. They drew to a halt opposite the small half-timbered building used as a headquarters of the local watch. They tethered their horses to the large rings set in the wall of the building and strode inside. Jonathan Smyth was a well-known, powerful figure in most of the county of Devon. The watch sergeant saw him coming in through the door and stood to attention behind his rude desk. 'Good morning, sir.' Smyth acknowledged the man and indicated for him to remain seated. 'What can I do for you, sir?'

'Drop the "sir" for a start. I trust you have heard of the ransacking, looting and probably murders in at least two areas not ten miles from here?'

'Indeed I have, sir, sorry, your...' He fumbled for a title to address his superior. 'I have already been to Dunscombe early this morning. I didn't call and see Squire Brassington because I wanted to return back here and organise reinforcements. I have sent one of my men on a fast horse to Exeter to seek extra armed men.'

'Good man,' responded Smyth. 'You have acted as I would expect. I stayed overnight at Squire Brassington's, and I can tell you the raid has injured him. Now, how soon do you expect to get your extra men and how can we assist your endeavours? We are five strong, all armed and at your disposal.'

The watchman obviously did not know how to

answer Jonathan; he did not know how long the machinery of his masters' bureaucracy would take. 'I honestly do not know, err ... my lord, sorry.'

Smyth had been very tolerant with the man. Now his patience was ebbing away. 'Look here, while your superiors sit around large tables and discuss if and how many men they will send here, people's lives and homes are in danger. I cannot stand around and wait while help comes. I intend raising a militia. Good morning.' With that he spun on his heels and strode out into the weak morning sunshine, Tom following close on his heels.

Outside Smyth turned to Tom and said, 'It seems to me that we may be on our own resources for some days. Mount up and let's get back to our men.'

Chapter 3

Back on the edge of Dunscombe, Tom and Smyth dismounted and Silas led both horses to the nearby stream to let them drink.

'Well, I have to say we have achieved very little. The watchman has sent one of his men to Exeter to ask for reinforcements. They probably only have six men at arms to cover there own area. If I am correct, they will request that troops of the local army battalion be sent to take care of the brigands. It could take a week before they get here. In that time these villains will have ransacked and murdered whole families. I suggest we try to raise our own militia.'

Silas responded, 'Sir, where are we going to get enough men armed and willing to lay down their lives to get rid of these people?'

'I don't know. It occurred to me that if we could be sure the *Pegasus* was in port, they could assist us.'

Caleb jumped in. 'If they are in port, most of the crew will be spending a lot of time at the Eagle Tavern. I could ride down there and find out where they are. Somebody will know what their schedule is.'

'Caleb, that is a capital plan. Old Sammy Watson would be sure to know where the lads are, and he spends most of his life in the Eagle. You had better get underway.'

'What can we be doing in the meantime?' asked Tom.

Jonathan Smyth stroked his chin. 'Probably the best plan is to find where else these fiends have been already, and if they haven't raided any hamlet or village, tell the inhabitants to be prepared as best they can.'

Tom and James always addressed Jonathan Smyth by his first name when they were in each other's company. When they were with the rest of his staff or in mixed company, they would always address him as 'sir'. That was the respect they had for Jonathan Smyth. 'Sir,' Tom asked, 'can James and I ride out to some of the villages and gather information?'

Jonathan nodded his approval. 'Certainly, get Silas to see that you have enough arms. Be back at Windfell Manor by nightfall. We are staying overnight there.'

Silas, Tom and James walked off towards where their horses were again grazing. Silas checked that both young men had a pair of loaded saddle pistols and that they each had plenty of pistol balls and powder. Each also carried a pair of flintlock pistols in leather holsters hung from their waist belts, together with a navy-type sabre. They mounted and Silas waved them off.

Jonathan cast his gaze to his remaining comrade. 'Well, I suppose we had better spend the rest of the afternoon riding west to see what we can gather.' The pair trotted off in what was left of the ebbing sunshine.

Chapter 4

By mid-afternoon Tom and James had visited two villages in the area. Any raids had not affected the inhabitants of each community. Tom and James told the village elders of recent events that had affected the other communities, and warned them to take precautions as best they could. They explained that their employer was attempting to raise a militia to stave off the brigands until the army could be brought into the area. They asked if any suitable volunteers for the militia would put their names forward. Eventually two men in their middle twenties said they would help, although they had no arms training.

The third hamlet had had news that a renegade band had ransacked two communities. They were preparing to protect their homes by sealing off the road into their hamlet using farm wagons blocked across the roadways. No volunteers came forward for duty.

Wearily, the two lads decided to head back for Windfell Hall. The late afternoon sun was now giving way to the oncoming evening sky. As the sun was slipping beyond the horizon, a distinct chill was coming over the land. Tom shivered slightly. 'Come on, Jim, I'm tired and cold, let's get back to Windfell.' The lads spurred their horses into a steady gallop.

They entered a heavily forested gorge, knowing that this short cut would get them back onto the main highway more quickly than the long road around the gorge.

'Hands high in the air!'

They spun around in the saddle to see where the command had come from. Two swarthy men were standing in the pathway they had just ridden across, both brandishing a pair of flintlock pistols. The darkest of the men was bearded. His long hair was pulled into a ponytail at the back of his head. The other man was unshaven and his greying hair was straggly and unkempt. Both men were dressed in a type of warm reefer coat, rough hemp trousers and dirty boots finishing halfway up their shins.

Tom's first instinct was to pull his pistol. The dark-haired man anticipated Tom's action. 'Don't be stupid, young'un, you'd be dead before you'd pulled it from your belt. Now get down off those animals and hand over your weapons.'

James looked to his front in response to a noise. Two more armed men were now blocking their escape. 'Obey, or we're both dead,' said James.

The lads dismounted and unbuckled their belts; they then put their hands in the air. Two men approached them and collected their swords and pistols. 'These two young'uns must belong to somebody important. They be well armed and well dressed.' The man was admiring Tom's heavy woollen riding coat and clean black thigh boots. The other men stepped forward now and began to examine both lads' clothing. 'Sons of a rich man, are ye?' Tom and James didn't answer. They just stared at the sky. 'Should fetch a handsome ransom,' said the bearded man.

With both the lads' wrists tied, the mystery men began to march them through the now dark forest.

One man was left heading up the rear, leading the two horses behind the party.

Tom and James occasionally tripped over loose branches on the forest floor. Tom estimated that they must have walked some two miles when he saw fires burning in the distance through the trees. Soon after, the group entered the clearing. They saw ten men in the clearing. Some were sitting by the log fire. Others were breaking tree branches or cleaning weapons. A crude form of cooking tripod was set up over the fire with some kind of meat roasting on it. Glancing about them, Tom and James came to the conclusion that this motley band was some gang of outlaws.

'Who are you, and what do you want from us?' asked James.

The bearded man sniggered. 'It'll all be depending how much you be worth. If you turn out to be worthless, you'll die.' With that he walked over to the fire to warm himself.

Jonathan Smyth and Silas had reached Windfell Manor and were warming themselves in front of the large fire in the great hall in the manor house. 'It is late, I would have expected Tom and James to be here by now,' said Jonathan.

'Aye, sir, I would think they must have been struggling with the darkness. It must be slow travelling.' Jonathan said he was going up to his friend's bedchamber to ask after his progress.

It was a half hour later when he descended the stairs. 'Have Tom and James arrived yet?'

'No, sir.'

'I am really worried now, but I can't think what we can do. We don't even know where they could be.'

Chapter 5

Caleb had safely arrived at Bascombe, the small port that the *Pegasus* used when it came into shore. He stabled his horse in the town stable and made his way down the dark main street towards the Eagle Tavern. A warm glow, laughing and chattering came from the interior as he opened the inn door and entered. The inn was half full. A warm, smoky atmosphere greeted him. He carefully wandered round both rooms, looking for a recognisable face. Eventually he saw the character he was hoping to see.

'Sammy, how are you keeping, you old rogue?'

'Caleb, my old shipmate. It's been a while since I espied you.'

The two sat down together and Caleb ordered two tankards of ale. 'What are you doing in port, Caleb? I heard that you were working for Jonathan Smyth.'

'I still am. I have travelled all this way to find out when the *Pegasus* will be back in port.'

Old Sammy stroked his grey hair and a puzzled look appeared on his face. 'Why would you be a-wanting to know that?'

'It's urgent, we need their help.'

Caleb decided that he had no option but to tell Sammy the whole story.

When Caleb had finished his narration, old Sammy looked shocked. 'I hadn't heard of these marauders. They must have concentrated further up the coast.'

Caleb nodded his agreement. 'Well, the *Pegasus* sailed out from here a week last Tuesday. I was a-talking with Josh, he's the skipper now, you know. They were a-taking a shipment of goods to Portugal. Josh reckoned they would be back in port sometime this week.'

'Should be back here by the weekend, then?' asked Caleb.

'Yes, I reckon you be about right.' Caleb fetched Sammy and himself another tankard of ale each. When he returned he informed Sammy that he had got himself a room for the night at the tavern. The pair then spent the rest of the evening chatting and drinking.

The bearded member of the gang that had captured Tom and James walked over to the big tree where both lads were tied up to. He released the ropes binding them to the tree. 'We can't be letting you two lads starve now, can we? You can come into the middle and eat. I'll tie your ankles together, but you can have your hands free till you have finished eating.'

After the meal came the questioning. 'Who are you? Where do you live? What were you doing out in the forest at that time?'

Tom gave James an unseen nudge and indicated with his eyes to keep quiet. The bearded man signalled to one of the men to take retributive action for the boys' silence. He kicked Tom hard on his legs. The bearded man grinned. 'Silence is not something we take kindly to when I ask a question.' He repeated his questions. Still the two sat, not responding.

The man moved on James this time and delivered a sharp kick into James's side. James winced; his ribs had taken the full blow. 'The next time I shall have a part of you cut off. Say a finger?' The last thing Tom or James wanted was to start losing limbs, and they did not doubt that they would carry out their threats.

Tom spoke, 'Tom Bascombe, and my friend is James Purdy.'

'And where are you from?'

'Kingsport.'

A huddle between one of the gang and the bearded man took place.

'My mate here reckons you be lying.'

Tom responded. 'Why would we lie?'

The bearded man said, 'Cause Kingsport is many miles from here, and you couldn't have got home in time.'

'But we were planning to stop over at an inn,' answered Tom.

The bearded man shrugged his shoulders. 'I'm tired. Tie them up and tomorrow we'll take them to the ship.' Tom glanced at James with a worried look. They now realised who had captured them.

Chapter 6

Silas took the broad stairway up to Jonathan Smyth's bedroom as quickly as he could. He banged on the bedroom door. 'Come,' answered the voice within.

'Sir, Tom and James are still not here. I checked their room and then with the squire's servants.'

Smyth looked very worried. 'If anything has happened to those two I shall never forgive myself. In hindsight we should have remained together. I shall dress. Meanwhile, get the horses ready.'

Silas took the steps down two at a time. He was out at the stables preparing the horses as Caleb came riding into the stable yard.

'What a welcome sight you are Caleb. You'd better get some breakfast while I saddle up a fresh horse for you.'

'Why, what's the fuss about?'

'Tom and James didn't get back here last night. Master is rightly worried that some ill may have come to them.'

Comprehending the urgency of the situation, Caleb dashed over to the kitchen to get himself some food. In the hallway he ran into Jonathan Smyth. 'Silas has told me about the two young'uns, sir. He is saddling a fresh horse, and I am about to get a bite to eat and then we can go.'

'Thank you, Caleb. Be as quick as you can. You can tell me what you have discovered as we ride.'

Some twenty minutes later the trio was trotting down the dirt road away from the manor house. The morning was cloudy, so it was warmer than it had been of late. Smyth cast his eye up at the sky. 'Well, at least if Tom and James had to sleep outdoors last night, it wasn't frosty.'

Caleb told Smyth about his meeting with Sammy Watson and that the *Pegasus* should be in port some time during the weekend, and that he asked Sammy to get word to them that Smyth was in urgent need of their help.

Silas said, 'Where are we going to start looking for the lads, sir?'

'We know two of the villages they intended going to. I propose we begin there and ask questions and see what we can discover.'

On entering the first of the villages the trio split up to ask any of the villagers if they had seen the two lads. It was nearly an hour later that a triumphant Silas called the other two to him. 'One of the market men remembers seeing Tom. He noticed him because of his expensive riding coat and high black boots.'

'Did he speak to him?' asked Jonathan.

'No, but he has told me a name and address of someone he did speak to.'

'Good, let's go and see him.' The three men strode down the main street. Smyth rapped smartly on the rough timbered front door of a whitewashed cottage. Eventually a white-haired old man opened the door. He was dressed in a worn coat with a clean but tatty cravat at his neck.

'Good day to you, sir,' said Jonathan Smyth. 'We have reason to believe you spoke to one of my men yesterday. We think he told you about getting prepared for any future raids by some renegades roaming this area.'

The old man's face lit up. 'Yes, sir, I recall your man. He came to me because I am the village elder and organise the affairs in the community.'

'I am here, sir, because they have not reported back to me and I am anxious to find him and his friend.'

The old man invited them into his cottage. 'He told me about these bandits that have been raiding and advised me what precautions we should take. Men are currently building barricades at one end of the village now. When they have done that, they will move to the end you came in on.'

'That's good. Can you tell me where they were going to after your village?'

'I remember him saying they were heading towards Chadfield.'

Smyth thanked the old man profusely for his help. Remounting their horses, they left the village at a smart trot heading towards Chadfield.

Two hours later they arrived in the small community. Again they split up to ask around. One of the trio was again directed to one of the village elders. The elder remembered the lads and directed them onto another community nearby.

At the third hamlet quite a few recalled seeing the distinctive pair. Two of the young men told Smyth that they had offered their names up for militia duties. No one knew where Tom and James were headed when they left them. Smyth thanked them all for their help.

'Well, sir, what do we do now?' asked Silas. Jonathan Smyth half turned in the saddle and fished out a linen map from his saddlebag. He studied it for some minutes while the other two watched in silence.

'Well, looking at this map it appears we are quite a distance from the main road that would take us back to the manor. There is a gorge of some sort not far from here. If there is a track through the gorge, that would be a considerable short cut to the main highway.'

'So you think Tom and James may have taken that short cut?' asked Silas.

'I definitely think it is worth a visit.'

The three spurred their horses into a gallop and headed towards the gorge.

Half an hour later they were entering the heavily forested valley. They brought their steeds to a walk, scanning the forest floor at each side of the rough path. After moving a few hundred yards along the path, Smyth brought his comrades to a halt. He jumped down from his horse and scanned the ground to his right. 'Look here, lads, I think there may have been some kind of a scuffle.'

With all three horses tied to a tree, the three men searched the area for evidence of misdemeanours.

'Sir, over here.'

'What have you found, Caleb?' Smyth made his way quickly over to Caleb, who was holding a button.

'This is a button off one of the lads' riding coats.'

Smyth handled the button. 'Undoubtedly it is. Search some more. We may find some more clues.'

A bit later Silas discovered an overgrown pathway that had most of its plant life broken and bent over. 'Someone has been through here recently. Let's see where this leads us.'

Smyth asked Caleb to fetch the horses. Minutes later all three were carefully walking the pathway, all the time looking for further clues.

They made their laborious way forward for over an hour. Eventually they emerged into a clearing. Smyth and Silas looked at each other. 'Quite a few men have used this place as a camp site. Look here, remnants of wasted food, ashes from a fire, bushes and plants all broken. It all looks very recent to me,' responded Silas.

'Yes. I think there is very little more we can do here today.' Smyth looked up at the dull, sunless sky where the remaining daylight was abandoning itself to an early darkness. 'I say we head back to Windfell Manor while we can still see where we are going. We can come back here in the morning and see if there is more to discover.'

Darkness had secured its full grip by the time Smyth and his men rode into the stable yard. Jonathan left Silas and Caleb to take care of the horses. As he entered the entrance hall, Mistress Brassington spotted him. 'Ah, Jonathan, my husband has been able to get up from his sick bed today. He asked if you would care to join him in the main hall. I will send in some refreshments.'

Jonathan smiled and thanked her. He entered the large wood panelled hall. George Brassington was seated in a large winged chair besides a generous fire burning in the great hearth.

'George, it is good to see you up and about. I trust you are feeling better?' George was still wearing a bandage about his head and looking a little pale, but Jonathan could see a marked improvement in his demeanour.

'Yes, thank you, I feel a great deal better now. Come and sit down and tell me what you have discovered to date.'

Jonathan Smyth spent the next twenty minutes telling his friend all that had happened. George looked sad and said, I am very sorry to hear about Tom and James going missing. I hope you find them soon. You care a lot about those two, don't you?'

Smyth looked sad and said, 'Yes, I do. I am hoping that one day they may take my place and manage my estates. After the death of my wife I swore to myself that I could never marry again: I could never love another as I loved her. It follows that I will never have children. When I met those two gutsy boys, I knew I could teach them to carry on when I am dead and gone.'

'Oh, come now, you are still young enough to find a suitable lady to marry and settle down with.'

Jonathan shook his head. 'I cannot envisage that, my friend.' He changed the subject quickly. 'I have told the watch at Exeter to leave a message here as soon as he can get me some armed assistance.'

'I only wish I were well enough to help you,' said George. 'I think you have already seen enough of these marauders. Ah, food has arrived and I am very hungry.'

Chapter 7

That same day Tom and James had been forced marched miles through forests until eventually they emerged at Aston Creek. Here, the tree-covered hills dropped steeply down the gorge sides into a small, concealed beach. The sea inlet was deep enough to harbour a ship and at the same time conceal it from prying eyes. It was an ideal hiding place for a pirate ship or a smuggling ring. The added advantage was its isolation from any township.

'These people must be the raiders we've been trying to trace,' said Tom to James.

'Shut up the both of you,' bawled the bearded man.

After scrambling down a narrow winding pathway between the trees, the small group descended over a hundred feet to the narrow beach.

'Fetch the longboat from the bushes, Sol.' Two men immediately obeyed and went off into a patch of shrubs. Minutes later Tom and James were being rowed out to a three-masted sailing bark swaying gently at anchor in the creek.

They were hauled aboard and pushed towards the rear cabin area of the ship. A door opened. A tall, slender man stood in the doorway. He had salt-and-pepper hair, which was set in a short ponytail at the back. He was dressed in a cream shirt, which had been white when it was new. The cravat about his neck was the same colour. His black trousers had been rubbed smooth with wear. His knee-length boots had not seen polish for a considerable length of time.

'And who have we here, Jim?'

The bearded man gave a curled fingered salute to his captain. 'They'd a-been asking questions about us, and as they looked well turned out, I captured them. Thought as how we could get a good ransom for 'em.'

'And do you know where they come from?'

'No, Captain, I only know their names. I reckon we can work on that here.'

The captain sniggered. 'Put them down below. I'll find that out later.'

That night some fifty men set out from the pirate ship to make a devastating raid on the nearby village of Beddington. During the night they burnt the village community hall down to the ground, ransacked a lot of homes and stole any treasure they could find. Three men who dared to challenge them were cut to pieces, and their bodies were left in the street. A number of fires were left blazing in houses as they finally rode out of the village and back to their ship. The terrible news spread throughout the neighbouring townships the following morning.

Jonathan Smyth, Silas and Caleb finished a hasty breakfast and saddled up their mounts to ride out to the spot they had found the rough encampment the day before. On their way they rode into the first village on the route to find an excited group. A large number of people knew the face of Smyth because of his banking and lending business in the area. As they saw him entering the village, one man waved his arms to attract his attention. 'Sir, have you heard the terrible news?'

The three men reined their horses to a stop. 'What news?'

'The raiders struck Beddington last night. They murdered three men.'

'Good God.' Smyth turned to Silas and Caleb. 'I think we should make our way there right away. Thank you for telling us. Make your community as safe as you can. Block the roads in and out,' he told the group gathered round them.

It was a scene of utter devastation that the three men witnessed as they entered the village. After walking round the area and talking to some of the village inhabitants, Jonathan said to his comrades, 'We have to find these people, and quickly.' He took the linen map from his saddlebag and scanned it. 'These men have got to be camped somewhere in the area, but I'm not sure where to begin. We could use a lot more help.'

Silas had been thinking about the problem. 'What if they didn't need a camp?'

Smyth looked puzzled. 'Go on, explain yourself. You obviously have something on your mind.'

'Well, sir, I was wondering what if they had a ship? A ship would act as a base and a warehouse for their plunder.' A grin spread across Smyth's face.

'Silas, you may have hit upon the truth. I thought these renegades were landlubbers. As you say, it is more likely they could be ship-based, which would make it easier to get away.'

He scanned the map once more looking for suitable inlets. After a few minutes he told his comrades, 'There are three possibilities where a ship could be moored. One is at Smithies Reach, then Aston Creek and finally at Kingsdown.'

Silas held out his hand for his master to hand him the map.

Once Silas and Caleb had finished scanning the map, Smyth said, 'Well, which should we try first?'

Silas was the first to answer. 'Aston Creek is the nearest.'

When they arrived at the wood overlooking Aston Creek, they dismounted, tied up their horses and made their way through the trees to a point where they could look down on the inlet. 'There is a ship down there,' exclaimed Jonathan Smyth. Silas and he immediately extended their telescopes to gaze down at the vessel. 'There is no sign of life on the ship.'

Silas concurred with his master.

'I would think that someone would be wandering about the deck,' said Smyth.

Silas and Caleb agreed that at least someone was expected to either be on watch or busy doing some task or other.

'If this is the ship we are looking for, we would be foolish getting any nearer, as we are only three men. We should keep a lookout overnight and discover if anybody returns to the ship. How we could use our friends from the *Pegasus* right now,' said Smyth.

Caleb jumped in, 'Sir, I would be happy to keep watch overnight. I was also thinking that we couldn't be too far away from Bascombe Harbour. If I see signs of anything suspicious, I could ride to Bascombe and see if the *Pegasus* has docked.'

'Good man, Caleb. Take my telescope.' Smyth then took out his map. 'Bascombe is about twenty-five to thirty miles east of here. If you take the road we came here on and head south it will get you there. Silas and myself will take a look at the other inlets and then head back to Windfell Manor. Keep out of sight and we shall wait for you here tomorrow. Goodnight Caleb.'

Chapter 8

Tom and James were tied in a sitting position to one of the masts in the ship's hold. They had witnessed various goods being brought on to the ship, consisting of good-quality furniture, linens, silks and household items.

'These men must have made a raid on some poor villagers and left them in a sorry state,' said Tom.

'Tom, I have been working away at my ropes, and I may soon be free.'

'If we can get ourselves free, we can escape while the pirates are collecting their loot.'

'Well, we can't hear any noise,' replied James.

Minutes later James had a free hand. He busied himself loosening his other hand, then his feet. He then hurried round to where his friend was bound. Tom's ropes had been fastened more professionally, and James had difficulty untying the bindings. He looked round the hold and discovered a small axe on a barrel. 'Be careful not to make a noise with that axe,' said Tom. James rubbed the blade against the thick ropes, rather than chopping at them. Eventually he freed Tom.

The two lads crept towards the wooden stairway leading to the next deck up. Carefully and quietly making their ascent, Tom poked his head over the floor level of the next deck. He waved his friend to follow him, putting a finger to his closed lips, signalling him to remain quiet. It seemed very odd that the pirates had left the ship deserted. They wouldn't rely on their instincts, however; they would assume that somebody was aboard the vessel. Tiptoeing along the deck, they found the next stairway that would take them to the main deck and daylight.

There was a scuffle of feet. Tom spun on his heels to see a tall, thin man bearing down on him, a dagger was raised above his head in his right hand. 'You whelp, you will die!' Tom had the presence of mind to sidestep at the final moment. The body of the man collided with the wooden stairway. James leapt upon the man and began raining blows upon his head. The pirate lashed out frantically with the dagger. The sharp blade ripped into James's shirtsleeve and blood appeared on his arm. Tom took a mighty kick at the crouching man. The stunning blow caught the man in the ribs. He fell to the floor and without another moment's hesitation, Tom delivered another massive kick to the man's head. The man lay lifeless on the deck.

'Are you all right, Jim?'

James examined his bleeding arm. 'It hurts a lot, but it doesn't feel as though it went deep.' He ripped the end of his sleeve off and Tom wrapped it round his wound like a crude bandage. 'If there is anyone else on board, they must have heard that commotion,' said Tom.

Tom was right: they had been heard. Two more men came clambering down the wooden stairway, the first bent low to see what the noise was about. Tom reacted instantaneously. He leapt over to the companionway and grabbed the man by his head and yanked him headways down the stair. The man lay in a crumpled heap at the bottom, struggling to right himself. James quickly saw the situation and ran over to take on the second man hovering at the top of the stair. The man started down the stair with a large dagger in his right hand. James quickly scanned the area round him for a weapon. He saw a small piece of netting and dragged it towards him as the man started a speedy descent. The man, now almost on the bottom step, took a lunge towards James. James swung the net towards the flailing blade. It caught the man's dagger hand and part of his body. James pulled at the man's descending body. The impetus brought him down on the deck.

Meanwhile Tom was struggling with the other man. He was beating him about his head, missing him more often than he landed a blow. The man was starting to get to his feet. Tom saw a small empty barrel. He picked it up and hit the struggling man with it. The man fended it off with his arm. Tom stood back and quickly took another swing with the barrel. This time it hit the man fair and square in his face, and he collapsed in a heap.

Tom looked over at his friend to see if he could help. The two of them were struggling. Suddenly the man rolled over and then lay still, a broad-bladed dagger stuck deep into his chest. James got up off the deck and stood in astonishment. Both lads stared at what had happened. 'He's dead!' exclaimed Tom.

'I didn't do it.'

'Well, he must have rolled onto his own blade,' said Tom.

'Anyhow, he's not a problem any more. Let's get the other two tied up before they recover,' said James.

That done, they emerged onto the main deck and daylight. 'I can't understand why nobody else seems to be around.'

'Yes, it does seem odd,' replied James.

They jumped over the side and swam for the nearby shore. On the shore they quickly found cover among the many trees and lay there to get their breath back.

What they didn't know was that the majority of the crew including the pirate captain, were busy transferring the plunder from their previous night's raid to the ship. That morning some of the crew had stolen a carthorse and cart from a local farm and taken it to where the crew had hidden the plunder. It was sheer luck that Tom and James had been able to make their escape at this point in time.

Jonathan Smyth and Silas had made their way to Smithies Reach and then on to Kingsport, only to discover that there were no big vessels harboured there. All they saw were rowing boats or small fishing boats at anchor. The afternoon was now giving way to the early evening gloom. 'Let's head for the nearest village and find a tavern to stay for the night,' said Jonathan.

Meanwhile Caleb settled himself down for his night's vigil. He didn't know that he and his two comrades had already missed the action of Tom and James escaping from the *Saracen*. He took his heavy riding coat from his horse's saddlebag, wrapped it around himself and settled himself down in a spot high up on the tree-lined hilltop, from where he could see onto the main deck of the ship.

He had less than one hour to wait. He could hear the noise of approaching men together with the rumble of cartwheels. He couldn't see anything from his position, but the noise was fairly near. His horse was tethered a good way away from where the din was coming from. He stayed quiet and waited. Eventually he witnessed some of the crew of the ship struggling down the narrow steep pathway to the shore. They were lugging large boxes of something. A series of curses rent the air as one of the wooden boxes slipped away from the men and rolled down the path. It splintered into pieces, and bright metal, clothing and silks tumbled down through the woods towards the shoreline. Caleb put the telescope to his eye and monitored the chaos. 'That looks like the spoils of a raid to me,' he said to himself.

Men began running about between the trees picking up the cascading items, whilst the rest of the crew continued their task of getting the remainder down the steep pathway. Caleb calculated that it must have taken the pirates over three hours to get the plunder from the cart onto the ship. He was now convinced that these were the men that Jonathan Smyth wanted to capture. He judged that to stay in his observation position would be somewhat pointless; he would be better employed riding to Bascombe to see if the *Pegasus* had arrived in dock. Furthermore, an early frost was starting to settle on the ground and it would be warmer having a bed at an inn. He gathered his belongings together and made his way quietly towards his tethered horse. Minutes later he was trotting along the track that Smyth had told him would meet up with the highway that would lead him to Bascombe.

Chapter 9

Tom and James lay in the dense foliage of the bracken and trees, out of sight of any sharp-eyed individual. They had moved as far away from the ship as possible and decided that they could use the little amount of heat left in the afternoon sun to get themselves a bit drier.

'Listen, what's all that noise?' said James.

Tom jerked his head up from his recumbent position to listen. 'Sounds as though it's some of the crew returning.'

The next sounds they heard were the crashing and banging of items cascading down the steep pathway, then loud cursing from gruff voices.

'Keep your head down. It would be a real disaster if we were recaptured now,' whispered Tom. They were quite a way from the path so they should be safe if they stayed hidden.

The commotion and shouting seemed to go on for ages. Eventually things got quieter. Tom peered through the bracken to see if there were any stray crew wandering round. 'Let's go up the slope towards the hilltop,' murmured James. Tom nodded his agreement and the two lads stealthily crept through the thick bracken as far away from the path as possible. It was ironic that whilst Caleb had been scanning the valley with his telescope he had noticed a disturbance in the bracken on the opposite side of the valley. He thought it must be animals.

114

The pirate captain, Jacob Watson, almost had an apoplectic fit when he boarded his ship and saw one of his crew with a dagger protruding from his chest and two more men tied up and bleeding.

'What the hell happened here? And where are the prisoners?'

One of the trussed men blurted out, 'Cap'n, we were jumped on. They seemed to come from nowhere.'

'Who came from nowhere? There were only two damned prisoners, and they were only just at shaving age.'

'There must have been about six of 'em,' the man lied. He dare not tell his ruthless master the truth: he had seen better men than him receive a cutlass thrust into their ribs for less incompetence than their own.

Watson flew further into a rage and took his temper out on any crew that was near. 'Stay away from him until he cools down,' was the warning that went round the crew.

The twilight turned to darkness. This made it far easier for Tom and James to make their getaway. Finally they were on top of the steep hillside looking down onto the *Saracen*.

'Which way shall we go?' said Tom. James looked up to the sky and saw the frosty moon. He scanned the horizon for any glimmer of daylight left. Deep on the skyline he saw some brightness.

'I reckon that must be west.'

Tom looked over to where James was pointing. 'Yes. So?'

'Well, I think we should walk north, which must be that way.' He pointed in the appropriate direction. Tom just nodded and both lads set off walking.

After two hours tramping through the forest, a field came into view. 'A cultivated field spells civilisation, and civilisation means food, and I am famished,' said Tom.

'So am I,' replied James.

They hurried across the field and climbed the crude fence on the other side. Two more fields later a small farmhouse came into view. Lights were flickering in two of its windows. Tom approached the front door and rapped on it. A large, dark-haired man opened the old door. His presence filled the opening.

'Yes, what can I do for you?'

'Sir, we are cold and very hungry and have escaped from a pirate ship moored at Aston Creek. Please take pity on us.'

The big man stared at the two young men for some time. It seemed like hours to the two lads. Eventually he stood to one side and motioned for them to enter.

'Aston Creek, you say. They wouldn't be they renegades that attacked Beddington last night, would they?'

Tom stood shivering in the entrance to the cottage. 'I can only assume so, sir. They captured us two days ago and marched us to their ship. Today after we escaped we witnessed them loading plunder onto the ship. Our master is Jonathan Smyth, and we were tracking these villains when we split up to cover more ground. But we were waylaid by these men and captured.'

'Come by the fire and get warm. My wife will prepare you some food. I reckon it will be only bread and cheese, but I don't think you'll be complaining.' Both lads thanked the farmer profusely.

As they munched through the bread and cheese,

the farmer said, 'I was in two minds to believe your story until you mentioned your master. It was Mr Smyth who lent me money to pay off a debt I owed. I tell you he was the only man who had faith in me. He is a good man.'

Tom smiled, 'Yes, sir, he has been very good to us these past six years. He took us in and treated both of us like his sons.'

After their meal Tom and James told the farmer about their experiences with the pirates and their quest to bring them before the law.

'I suppose you will be wanting some horses to get you back,' said the farmer.

'Yes, sir. Have you any idea where we can obtain any?'

The farmer rubbed his chin in thought. 'I have only a horse who is ageing a bit. He pulls my cart. I share two shire horses with my neighbouring farm to pull the plough and suchlike.'

'Oh, we wouldn't want to impose on you more than we have already. We would like directions to the nearest town,' said Tom.

'Oh, I can do better than that. The nearest town is Cressington, and it's a tidy step from here. You sleep on this here floor tonight, and in the morning I'll rig the horse up to my cart and take you to town.'

'Thank you very much, sir. We shall tell our master of your kindness when we see him next,' answered Tom. The farmer smiled and fetched the lads some rough woollen blankets.

It was very dark by the time Caleb reached Bascombe. He walked his horse down the main street towards the harbour front. He scoured the harbour for signs of the *Pegasus*, but it wasn't there. His disappointment was obvious from his slumped shoulders. He made his way back towards the Eagle Inn, but first he made sure his horse was comfortably stabled for the night. He then pushed open the oak door. Warmth, chatter and laughter greeted his ears and senses. He scanned the room to see if old Sammy was there.

'Why wasn't he here?' he thought.

The landlord greeted him and took him up to a room. 'I'll prepare you some food, say twenty minutes?'

'Before you go, have you seen Sammy this evening?'

'He may be in later.' With that the innkeeper shuffled down the stairway to organise some food for his guest.

Caleb had just finished his platter of stew and bread when Sammy entered the inn. 'Hello, Caleb, what brings you here so soon?'

'We are desperate for our old shipmates, and I wondered if they had come into port.'

'All I knows is they are due any time now.'

Caleb shrugged. 'Cap'n Smyth expects me back on my watch in the morning, so I must leave early.'

'Well, I told you I would get word to them as soon as they dock,' said Sammy.

The following morning Caleb rose early and dressed, then hurried down to the dock to scour the skyline. Nothing. He sat on one of the capstans, wondering what next to do for the best. On the horizon he thought he could see some sails. The early morning sun was catching something. He pulled out his telescope and focused it on the line where the sea met the sky. It was a ship. He was now in a bigger quandary. Should he wait and see if it was the *Pegasus*, or should he ride out to meet Jonathan Smyth, who would be riding to Aston Creek to meet with him and expect him to be there? He decided to wait.

A half-hour later Caleb lifted his telescope to his eye once more and let out a cry of joy, 'It's the *Pegasus.*' The odd fisherman must have thought he was crazy, but he didn't mind.

Smyth and Silas were cantering steadily along the highway heading towards the turn-off that would take them to Aston Creek. The morning was fine with high cloud, but it was cold.

'Silas, I am really worried about Tom and James. Two days and we haven't heard a thing. I wonder if Caleb has any news for us?'

'I hope so, sir.'

They dismounted near to where they left Caleb the previous evening, and tethered their steeds to graze on the grassy bank. They looked around to find their comrade. 'Where the blazes is he?' murmured Smyth.

Silas shook his head, 'He must have left for something important.'

'I just hope he is safe,' responded Jonathan.

They crept near the edge of the steep embankment and lay flat on their stomachs. 'The ship is still moored down there. Do you suppose Caleb saw something that made him leave?'

Silas looked at his master. 'You may have it there, sir. He probably saw something that sent him to Bascombe. If you recall, he did suggest that it would be best he went there at some time.'

Jonathan nodded that he remembered that. They decided that they had no other option than to lay concealed overlooking the ship lying at anchor in the bay.

Some time later they witnessed activity aboard the ship. Men began scurrying about cleaning decks, tidying and stacking ropes. After a while of this activity they realised why. 'Look down there, Silas. He must be the captain.'

Emerging from the rear cabin quarters of the ship, a tall, slim man strode onto the main deck and cast his eye up towards the sky. The sun was very weak in the scratchy cloud-streaked sky. Jonathan and Silas had their telescopes firmly fixed to their eyes. The captain was now gesticulating, his arms waving about, obviously pointing to various things about the ship. 'Well, if he ain't the captain, he certainly acts like,' sniggered Silas. Jonathan smiled at his comrade.

Chapter 10

Tom and James helped the farmer bring his horse and cart from his stable and attach the reins. The two lads thanked the farmer's wife for her hospitality and jumped aboard the cart, and the farmer urged his horse forward. 'Come on, Bob, let's go.'

The eager horse trotted out of the farmyard and out onto the track road towards Cressington. It was just over ten miles to the town. Bob made the journey in just over two hours.

As the trio entered the township the farmer made a slight diversion into a side street off the main road. 'Here, lads, there's a place down here which may be to your advantage.' He called for Bob to halt. The lads looked around, wondering what on earth he was meaning.

'Look there, Tom, a Mercantile Farmers' Bank.'

Tom's eyes lit up. It was one of the bank branches owned by Jonathan Smyth.

Tom and James jumped down from the cart and thanked the kind farmer for all his help. They entered the bank and asked one of the clerks if they could see the manager. 'And who shall I say wishes to see him?' said the clerk, looking disparagingly at the two unkempt lads.

'Jonathan Smyth's wards,' responded Tom.

Two minutes later an elderly man, bald on top but with bushy sideburns, walked from his office doorway.

His face had a glimmer of recognition on it. 'Ah yes, I have seen you two before. I remember you visited here with Mr Smyth on two occasions.'

Tom breathed a sigh of relief. 'I am Tom Bascombe and my friend is James Purdy. We are wards of Jonathan Smyth.'

'What can I do for you today?'

'If we could step into your office, we shall tell you all.' The manager ushered them into his inner sanctum and offered them a chair each.

Twenty minutes later Tom and James had narrated the whole story to the man, who sat back in his chair and looked amazed. 'What a harrowing experience you have suffered. But what do you require from me?'

Tom answered. 'Sir, we have to meet up again with Jonathan Smyth, and we have neither horses nor clothing. Also we could do with some weapons.'

The manager rubbed his hand across his forehead. 'I suppose Mr Smyth would be happy for me to let you have some money to buy your horses and clothing. I have a few pistols in my safe: your master likes to protect his money and his business and insists we keep weapons at each branch to fend off robbers. Now how much do you think you may need?' The three worked out the costs, and the manager left them alone while he went to the safe. Minutes later he was back with a small cloth bag and two large riding pistols which would normally be strapped to a horse's saddle.

'There is sufficient money in this bag for the purchase of two good stallions, money for clothing and some food. I suggest that you pick up these pistols when you are ready for leaving, as they are heavy to carry in your belts and you don't want to scare the local shopkeepers,' he grinned.

Back out in the street, James espied a general store and outfitters. Some time later they emerged from the shop transformed, with new breeches, shiny boots, dark brown long riding coats and tricorn hats. They strutted along the street in the direction of the town's stables, which was on the edge of the town. Twenty minutes or so later the two were again making their way down the main street back towards the bank, this time astride two beautiful black stallions.

They knocked on the manager's door and entered. 'My, what a transformation,' he said, looking up from the work on his desk.

'I'm afraid we have spent all the money you gave us. The stable man had two sabres that he let us have, so we have no money left.'

The manager put his hand into his purse and produced a few more coins. 'This should buy you some food for your journey. Good luck to you both, and give my best regards to Jonathan Smyth.' Tom and James thanked the man as they left.

'Well, where to from here?' asked James.

'I have been giving that some thought. Surely Jonathan, Silas and Caleb have discovered the *Saracen* anchored at Aston Creek by now. I say we ride there, but this time in utmost secrecy. To be kidnapped a second time would be very stupid.' They trotted out of the town and onto the highway.

Squire Brassington was interrupted from his task by the sound of marching men entering his courtyard. He dashed to the window to see some twenty-five red-coated soldiers come to a halt, and opened the main door to see an army captain walking towards him. 'Squire Brassington?'

'Yes.'

'We have been dispatched from our garrison in north Devon to assist you in capturing some renegades.'

'Well, it's not really me that is after these ruffians. My good friend Jonathan Smyth is currently on their trail. The problem is he only has four or five men with him. Furthermore, I am not sure where he is at the moment.'

'So what do you suggest we do, sir?' asked the young captain.

'I presume you have marched all the way here?' The captain nodded that they had. 'I have two large carts that should accept all of you. I will get some of my staff to get them ready, and I suggest you rest your troops and allow them to eat while this is being done. My men will take you to the last village that was ransacked and where I know Smyth was heading.'

Two hours later, two large farm carts with twenty-five infantrymen aboard were on their way towards Beddington.

Caleb waited excitedly on the harbour for the *Pegasus* to begin mooring.

'Hello, Caleb, my old shipmate. Are you after getting your old job back?'

Caleb laughed nervously. 'I wish it was that simple, Jeb. Where is Captain Josh?'

A large face appeared at the ship's side. 'Seems to me you have a problem, Caleb. Wait while we lower the gangplank and come aboard.'

Caleb dashed up the plank shook hands with Josh. Some of his old shipmates gathered round to listen. Caleb hurriedly related the events of the last few days. When he had finished Josh said, 'So where does Cap'n Smyth want us?'

'I am going to ride for Aston Creek. I hope that Captain Smyth and Silas are waiting for me there. It will take you some time to unload and get prepared. Head towards the mouth of the creek, but stay offshore, by tomorrow, and I will signal you from the headland.'

'Tell Cap'n Smyth we will be there,' responded Josh. With that, Caleb mounted his steed and made his way as quickly as possible for Aston Creek.

It was late afternoon when an exhausted horse carrying Caleb arrived at the edge of the creek. He tethered the horse near a small stream and left it to graze. Quietly he crept along the hilltop, making sure he was sheltered from watchful eyes by moving between the trees and approaching the spot where he took up yesterday's vigil.

'Shush, someone's coming,' whispered Jonathan Smyth. Both men lay flat on the ground, hidden by the thick bracken. Caleb stealthily moved within three feet of the prostrate men.

'Caleb!' He whirled round to see Silas looking up at him.

'Thank God you waited for me,' was Caleb's excited whispered reply.

'Tell us what you know,' said Jonathan's reassuring voice.

In a low voice Caleb described the events of yesterday, starting with the brigands loading their spoils onto the ship, and how that set him to find out if the *Pegasus* had arrived in port. He went on to tell of the morning's meeting with the crew of the *Pegasus*.

'What arrangements have you made with the captain?' asked Jonathan.

125

'The captain is old Josh Walker now, by the way,' responded Caleb. Jonathan and Silas raised their eyebrows at the news. Caleb continued, 'I asked them if they would sail the *Pegasus* round to this bay, but stand offshore till they received a signal from us. I also reminded them to have all their cannon at the ready. Josh reckoned he could have the ship within easy sight of us by tomorrow afternoon, as he has to unload their cargo first.'

Jonathan Smyth appeared satisfied at that. 'Good man, Caleb.'

The three decided to pool what provisions they had between them. They sat low down between the masses of bracken, whispering what to do now. 'I wish we knew where Tom and James were. I am really worried about those two,' said Jonathan. 'Seeing as there are only the three of us, we are going to have a great dependence on the lads from the *Pegasus*. It would be useful if we had some gunpowder.' Silas and Caleb looked at their master with surprise.

Chapter 11

It was late afternoon when Tom and James brought their horses to a stop on the highway just outside Beddington. 'Look over there. That looks like a small troop of soldiers.'

'Yes it is, and we certainly need them,' replied Tom. He reined his horse to his right and galloped over to where James had seen the troops.

'Excuse me, Captain, are you in search of the gang of brigands who raided this village?'

'Why do you ask?'

'We are headed where these men are. We are hoping that our master and some of his men are there also.'

The captain looked puzzled. 'How do you know where these bandits are, young sir?'

Tom smiled as he answered, 'We were captured by them but managed to escape.'

'And who is your master?' the captain asked.

'Jonathan Smyth, sir. We believe that there are at least fifty men aboard a ship anchored at Aston Creek. The ship is named the *Saracen*.'

The captain looked worried. 'Fifty men, you say. I have only twenty-five soldiers with me. So we would be outnumbered two to one.' He trotted over to where his sergeant was standing alongside his men. 'Sergeant, prepare the men for another journey. This time it will be a short one.' They climbed aboard the two carts once more, and the little band fell in behind Tom and James. It was a peculiar sight, the captain astride a black charger, leading his men, aboard two large hay carts, the whole band being led by Tom and James.

Aboard the *Saracen*, Captain Jacob Watson was briefing his two lieutenants on his plans for that evening. 'My scout has told me there is a rich little market town about eight miles from here. We will raid this place tonight, bring the plunder straight back on board and catch the morning tide out of here.'

His two men laughed. 'You certainly keep us wealthy, Jacob. We should go and organise our men for the raid,' said one.

'No more than twenty-five or thirty men on this trip. I shall stay aboard and make all preparations for sailing on the morning tide,' ordered Jacob Watson. The two men gave a curled-fingered salute to their captain and left his cabin.

Tom and James were now within half a mile of the ridge overlooking Aston Creek. Tom dismounted, handed his reins to James to hold his horse and walked back to where the Army captain had halted his troop. 'Sir, I suggest you leave your men here and walk the rest of the way to the ridge with us. We wouldn't want to give the pirates advance warning.' The captain agreed and dismounted. He gave his sergeant orders to keep the men quiet whilst he was away.

Fifteen minutes later the three were stealthily creeping along the eastern edge of the rim overlooking Aston Creek. 'Look, there are three horses tethered there,' said James in a hushed voice.

Tom acknowledged the sighting. 'You two stay here while I see who are the owners of these mounts.'

As he drew nearer to the horses, he recognised the saddles and saddlebags. 'These belong to Jonathan, Silas and Caleb,' he whispered to himself. Not wishing to fall into another trap, he continued to crawl along through the thick bracken. A few yards further along he heard hushed voices to his right. He edged nearer to where the hushed voices were coming from and carefully parted the bracken immediately in front of him. Sitting there were Jonathan, Silas and Caleb.

'All I can say is, it is lucky for you that I am not the enemy.'

The three men whirled round to face Tom peeping through the bracken. Their faces lit up. It was Jonathan who spoke first. 'Tom! Where have you been? Where is James? Oh, it's so good to see you.' He hugged him and Silas and Caleb patted him on the back.

'James is some yards back along with an Army captain. Why don't you come back with me and meet him?'

'We will, but keep down,' said Jonathan.

Minutes later Jonathan Smyth was shaking hands with the captain. 'It's good to see you, Captain. How many men have you here?'

The officer looked a little downcast before he responded. 'Sir, I am afraid our battalion commander could only spare twenty-five soldiers. I understand that these brigands are some fifty strong, which means we are still outnumbered.'

Jonathan placed a reassuring hand on the officer's shoulder. 'With some planning and good luck and the assistance from my old ship the *Pegasus*, we should easily apprehend these fiends.'

'The *Pegasus*?' queried the captain.

129

'Yes, she is a sturdy four-master equipped with twenty-five cannon and a very able and worthy crew. We have arranged for her to stand offshore and await our signal to move in. The problem is she will not be here till midday tomorrow.'

With that news the captain looked very pleased, but Jonathan had a frown on his face. 'Caleb, it would be a real sorry end if this ship slipped out of the creek on the high tide this day. It would mean all our efforts have been for nothing. Can you ride back to Bascombe and urge Josh to get here tonight?'

Caleb didn't question his master's reasoning. He saluted and sprinted away to get his horse and ride for Bascombe.

Jonathan now turned to the captain. 'Sir, I would recommend that you organise your own men to be as much camouflaged as possible. If this isn't carried out meticulously your troops will stand out in their red coats like a sore thumb, and our mission will be ruined.'

'Yes, sir, I will attend to that right away. My men will take up positions to the east and west ridges.' He came to attention and saluted smartly before hurrying off to give orders to his troop.

Jonathan turned to Tom and James. 'Now, tell me where you two have been.' The lads began their tale of the last three days. When they had finished, Jonathan said, 'I have to say that you both showed great initiative by going to one of my banks to seek the help of the manager. Well done.' He gave both lads a pat on their backs. 'It really is good to have you back with us.'

'Hear, hear to that,' said Silas.

'Now, let's get back to our observation on the ridge.'

Minutes later the four were settled in the thick bracken overlooking the *Saracen* laid at anchor in the creek below. After the captain had manoeuvred his troops into position, he made his way back towards where Jonathan, Silas, Tom and James were keeping watch.

'Captain, we can see where some of your men are supposed to be maintaining a low profile,' Smyth said sarcastically. 'I can see their red coats and their bayonets above the trees and bracken from here. Tell them to lie down with their muskets at their sides. We shall signal when they are required.' The officer slid away to remonstrate with his troops.

Twilight had given way to darkness when Caleb galloped down the main street and onto the dockside at Bascombe. He dismounted, tethered his horse and ran up the gangplank and onto the *Pegasus*. Josh met him as he boarded the deck. 'Back again, Caleb? I think you want your old job back.'

Caleb laughed. 'Captain Smyth told me to ask you if you could sail tonight. He has a suspicion that the pirates may make a break for it on the morning tide.'

'Well, it's lucky for you we completed the unloading earlier than I expected. We took the last casks off half an hour since. I checked our powder and shot, and we are ready for sailing if Cap'n Smyth wants us. We may as well go now while the tide is high.' He shouted down to the half dozen men on the dockside, 'All aboard, we're sailing now.' He turned back to Caleb. 'Are you sailing with us?'

'My horse is tethered down there.'

'Bring him aboard. It will give him a breather. We will drop you off at a suitable spot near the creek.'

Caleb dashed back down the gangplank to lead his mount onto the ship.

At Aston Creek everything remained quiet up on ridges overlooking the inlet where the *Saracen* was anchored. Smyth and his comrades were taking turns in keeping watch on the ship, while the others rested. A few lights glistened from the deck of the ship, but there was no movement.

Tom, on watch, yawned. His eye was suddenly drawn to a movement down on the main deck of the *Saracen*. Three or four men were walking across the deck. Hatches were being opened. Suddenly more men came into view. Tom nudged Jonathan Smyth from his slumbers. 'Sir, there is some action aboard the ship.'

Jonathan sat up, suddenly awake. He rubbed his eyes, took the telescope from Tom and adjusted the instrument to suit his own eyes and looked for a few seconds. 'There are over twenty men gathered on deck.' He peered through the telescope again for much longer. He had now caused the other two to waken with his quiet enthusiasm and shuffling about to obtain a better position to witness the scene taking place on the ship.

'What's happening?' whispered Silas?'

'A lot of the crew are on deck on the *Saracen*,' whispered Tom. Silas reached for his own telescope.

Jonathan removed the instrument from his eye and said, 'Unless I am wrong, a number of the crew are going ashore. They seem to be getting two long boats lowered into the sea.' Silas confirmed that they were all armed and making their way into the boats. Both telescopes were now scanning the ship's deck.

'Surely they are not making another raid,' exclaimed Jonathan. 'James, go and alert the officer, but tell him to make sure his men are quiet while getting into position.'

Jonathan and Silas continued to monitor the movements of the pirates, and Jonathan issued instructions to the captain. 'They are in the longboats, making their way to the bank. Let them come ashore, up the path and to the edge of the tree line, then have your men move on them from each side in a pincer movement. Whatever happens, don't let them get back to the ship. I cannot stress upon you enough that silence is paramount if we are to succeed.' The officer saluted and quietly moved off to his troops.

The pirates landed their boats up on the narrow beach and, thinking they were alone, noisily made their way up the narrow twisting pathway to the hill top. Muffled laughter brought a wince from Jonathan Smyth. 'What a disorganised rabble they are,' he whispered.

Silas smiled. 'In your time, you would have keelhauled the lot of them, sir.'

Jonathan gave a sly grin. 'Make sure all your weapons are loaded and ready,' he said to his friends.

Eventually the pirates congregated on the ridge top. Their lieutenant mustered them into a straggly formation and led them out through the trees and towards the narrow highway. 'Somebody's there,' shouted one of the pirates.

'Where are you looking,' shouted their leader.

'Charge!'

The pirate had seen the troopers too late. Soldiers bore down on them from both sides, bayonets attached to the ends of their muskets. One of the pirate gang quickly pulled out his pistol and fired. The ball hit a trooper in the middle of his chest and he fell to the ground dying. This action started a fierce firefight.

The troops already approaching the gang, with muskets levelled and instantly ready for use, opened fire. Several pirates fell to the floor from the salvo of musket balls.

Jonathan Smyth suddenly stood upright on hearing the noise from the salvo of gunfire. 'Come on, Silas, it sounds like the action has begun without us.' Tom and James also leaped to their feet.

'Now hold on, lads. Somebody has to stay and keep watch on the ship. You two stay here.'

Tom and James looked disappointed but understood. 'Don't worry, we will keep watch,' responded Tom. Jonathan and Silas dashed from their cover towards the fighting, each with a sabre in one hand and a pistol in the other.

On board the *Saracen*, Jacob Watson heard the distant shooting. 'What the hell is going on up there?' he shouted. He dashed to his cabin and returned within seconds with a telescope. Ranging the instrument up to the hilltop, he studied the scene. Frustrated by the darkness, he slammed the telescope down.

'What can you see, Captain?'

'Not much. All I can make out are flashes from guns. Troopers may have ambushed them. We have outstayed our time here. Get some men together and raise the anchor and unfurl the sails, and quickly.'

'But Captain, what about our lads up on the hilltop?'

'Don't be stupid! If there are a lot of soldiers up there, what chance do you think we would have? Or do you want to have your neck stretched on the gallows?' The seaman ran along the deck to get help.

* * *

When Jonathan and Silas reached the arena of the fighting they saw that about a third of the troopers were either dead or wounded. The pirates were in a slightly worse situation. The battle was now down to hand-to-hand combat. Smyth fired at one of the pirates and hit him in the neck. Blood gushed from the man's neck as he fell to the ground dead.

Silas fired his pistol and caught one of the villains in his left arm. The man reacted after the shock of the impact; he would feel the pain later. He surged at Silas with a broad, scimitar-like sword. Silas sidestepped, and the savage blade missed its intended mark. The pirate was now off balance. Silas took immediate advantage of this and his sabre came round on a horizontal plane to hit the pirate square in the middle of his back. The man howled with pain. Blood spurted from the large wound, and the man tumbled to the ground, never to get up again.

Smyth was now laying into the enemy with his sabre. He spotted the trooper captain facing two pirates. He was fending their blades off, but they were now tiring him. Smyth rushed to his side and immediately saw an opening in one of the pirate's guard. He thrust his sabre into the pirate's chest. The man gave out a terrible cry and fell. With renewed vigour the captain slashed at his other opponent and caught him a debilitating blow on his arm. The man ran off.

'Hold your attack,' shouted the lieutenant of the brigands. 'We surrender.'

'Hold your arms,' called the captain.

What was left of the troopers immediately ceased their onslaught. They stood where they were with muskets or sabres held at their foes. A quick head count revealed that from the original twenty-five soldiers in his command, the captain now had ten men left standing, four wounded and the rest dead.

He surveyed the pirate band. Of the twenty-seven men who started out on the fated raiding party, only seven were left standing, two badly wounded.

'Put these men in irons,' ordered the captain. He turned to Jonathan Smyth. 'You saved my life. Thank you.'

'You may have prevailed also, so I think any thanks should be just for any small assistance we may have given you.'

The captain gave a warm smile. 'I don't believe you know the meaning of small assistance, Baron. Your help has been immeasurable from my limited time involved in this venture.'

Tom came running onto the harrowing scene. 'Sir, the ship is preparing to leave. They are lowering their sails.'

'Right, let's go and see what is happening.' Smyth turned to the officer. 'When you have secured your prisoners, visit our lookout and we will update you.'

The officer sought his sergeant to give him orders. 'Are you badly hurt?' he asked him. He saw that blood was covering the side of the sergeant's face.

'No, sir, I received a blow from the butt of a pistol. I am able to carry on.' He removed his uniform cravat and wrapped it round his head to form a bandage.

The captain patted his sergeant on the shoulder. 'You and your men have done a very good job. Now we must tie these prisoners to the trees until we are ready to take them to jail.'

'Sir, two prisoners are badly wounded. What do you want me to do?'

The captain went to look at the two wounded men.

'Well, Sergeant, they don't look as though they will ever see the gallows. A pistol ball through their brains will be a mercy. Send a runner to Beddington to commandeer some hay carts.' The sergeant saluted. Seconds later two shots echoed through the trees.

Jonathan, Silas and Tom arrived back at their lookout. Excitedly James said, 'From what I can make out, it looks as though they have unfurled all their sails and are making ready to sail.'

Jonathan picked up the telescope. The darkness was making viewing difficult, but he could make out the outline. He turned to his friends. 'They have got to turn the ship round. They are at anchor, prow in towards the beach. They will need their longboats to pull the ship round, and two of those are still on the beach.'

At that moment the captain came up to them. 'Ah! Captain, just in time. Get your men down onto the beach and capture those two longboats. They will need them to tow the ship around to be able to sail. Stop them turning round and we have them.' The officer ran off to implement the order.

'Silas, get up to the headland and see if there is any sign of the *Pegasus*. If this goes wrong now, we shall lose these villains.'

The wind was now starting to blow up, parting the night clouds. The moonlight split what was now left of the evening clouds. This was probably the last thing the pirate captain wished to see. While there was complete darkness, he had some sort of secrecy.

The Army captain approached Jonathan Smyth. 'The rest of my able troopers are making their way down to the beach now.'

Minutes later, shots rang out. Jonathan put his telescope to his eye. 'Good God, some of the pirates have already reached the beach. They appear to have one of the longboats, and your men are firing at them.'

The captain picked up a spare telescope and focused it to his eye. 'Drat, the villains are getting away with one of the boats. My men have secured the other one.'

'Tom, James?' No response to Smyth's summons. 'Where have those two gone now?' was a question to himself.

Tom and James were scrambling as quietly as they could down the hillside near to where they had been located. They made their descent down through the trees and onto the narrow beach. Scrambling across the sand and shingle, they dived into the cold sea and swam with strong strokes towards the prow of the pirate ship, where a rope was hanging over the side into the water.

They hauled themselves up the rope and onto the front of the ship. Tom's head appeared above the railing. He looked about him to see if anyone was about. All the remaining crew seemed to be busy at the rear of the ship attempting to fasten securing lines to pull the ship round. Tom jumped over the rail and then helped James to scale the final few feet. As soon as they were on the deck they sprinted the few yards to where the anchor chain was secured.

'We need something heavy to knock this pin out,' said Tom. James searched round and found a metal bar. 'That will make a lot of noise, but we have no choice. Be prepared to make a quick getaway.'

Tom wielded the metal bar above his head and brought it down against the restraining pin. Clang! He repeated the action. Clang! The pin dislodged itself from its socket, and the anchor chain began rumbling through the metal hole in the ship. The heavy anchor hit the sea with a massive splash, and the chain continued to accelerate through the aperture until it had unrolled its full length on the hawser drum, which was bolted to the ship deck.

'What in great heavens is that noise?' cried Jacob Watson.

Two of the pirate crew who were working amidships heard the first of the clangs and ran along the deck to see what the racket was. Tom and James heard the heavy footfalls and ran to meet them head-on with sabres drawn. The first pirate saw what was happening and reached across his body to draw his cutlass. He was too late. Tom slashed at the man's right arm. A bright red spurt of blood gushed from the arm and he howled in pain. His sword was now useless.

The other pirate had anticipated the situation and was brandishing his sword. James parried the blow and with lightning speed brought his sabre back towards the man's chest. The blade went straight in between the man's ribs. He fell to the deck, dying. In the same instant, Tom brought his foot across the first pirate's head and kicked him as hard as he could.

'Right, over the side,' shouted Tom. Both lads dived over the ship's rail and struck out for shore.

Jonathan Smyth had watched part of this spectacle, not realising it was his wards who were causing mayhem. 'It seems some of the pirates are fighting among themselves,' he said to the captain. He looked more intensely through his telescope. 'Hell's teeth! I am not watching pirates fighting among themselves. Tom and James are battling them on their own ship. What do they think they are doing? They have dived into the water. Captain, can your men give them

139

some covering fire?' The trooper captain ran down the bank side, shouting his orders. Salvo after salvo of musket fire erupted from his men towards the *Saracen*.

Minutes later, Tom and James swam onto the beach and then, after catching their breath, made their way back to the hilltop.

'What the blazes do you think you were doing?' said an angry Jonathan Smyth. 'You could have been killed.'

Tom and James looked sheepish. 'We thought that if we dropped the anchor it would delay them for a good half hour. All the chain has fallen down with the anchor as well,' said Tom.

'It was a really brave thing to do, but if you had been killed, what would the wasted time have meant to me? Nothing.'

Chapter 12

On board the *Saracen*, Jacob Watson was purple with rage at having two of his enemy steal on board his vessel and drop the anchor. He wasn't concerned that he had one badly wounded and another one dead; his priority was that he and what was left of his crew should escape with their lives.

'Come on, get your backs into it and get that anchor raised. Mr Bosun, you make sure one of the men stands guard on the anchor when you have got it back up.'

'Aye aye, sir.'

He stormed off to the rear of the ship to urge the remainder of his men to pull hard on the longboat in order to pull the ship round to allow them to sail out of the creek. 'Get a move on, you slackers. Those troopers will have sent for reinforcements, and then we will be in trouble if we are still here. You won't want to be decorated with the hangman's noose, so get your backs into it.'

Silas stood on the headland, vainly searching the seas for his old ship, the *Pegasus*. His search was assisted by a moonlit sky. After an increasingly anxious wait for sight of the vessel, he thought he saw sails way off on the sea and focused his telescope. Yes, it was a sailing ship. Silas hoped that it was the right one.

The trooper captain had now mustered some of his remaining small band of troops into the captured longboat. Halfway between the beach and the *Saracen* he saw that the efforts of the pirate crew were slowly bringing results. The *Saracen* was being turned around to face out to sea.

'Aim at the men in the longboat. Make sure every shot counts,' were the officer's orders. A small salvo of musket shot went out from the troops on the longboat. Three pirates fell in the hail of shot.

'Get your heads down. Those damned soldiers are in our longboat and rowing towards us,' cried the pirate lieutenant.

A further hail of musket shot flew over the heads of the pirates. 'We're sitting ducks here. Pull alongside our ship and let us get aboard,' cried one of the men. The remainder of the longboat crew now backed him up.

'The ship isn't fully facing out to sea yet,' responded their leader. 'Just a bit more effort, then it's back to the ship.' The pirates pulled for their life on the long oars. Another hail of shot took a further pirate out of action. He slumped along the seat.

The *Saracen* was now almost facing out to sea. 'Right, back on board. Let's get out of this mess,' encouraged their lieutenant.

Jonathan Smyth was watching the situation down in the creek with increasing anxiety. What action should he take if the villains escaped, after all the effort he and his men had put in to attempt to capture them? Should he ask his old crew on the *Pegasus* to give chase and risk their ship and livelihoods, and possibly their lives? He was becoming more and more frustrated at seeing the pirate ship starting to slip from his grasp with little he could do about it.

Silas came running through the thick bracken, excited and breathless. 'Cap'n, it's the *Pegasus*, she is about a mile offshore and sailing in fast.'

Jonathan removed his hat and threw it on the ground with glee. 'Thanks be to God. We shall not be robbed of our capture.' He began running towards the headland, with Tom, James and Silas lagging far behind.

Tom said, 'I brought the lantern, as you forgot it.'

Jonathan laughed and patted Tom on the shoulder. 'Sometimes I dread to think how I would manage without both of you.' The lads looked at each other and laughed.

With the lantern lit, Jonathan signalled the *Pegasus* to move towards the mouth of the creek. Josh already had his telescope to his eye. 'Right lads, we're about to engage the enemy. Stand by the cannons. Bosun, steer us to the mouth of the creek but we stand offshore,' was his stern order.

Jacob Watson was the first to see the *Pegasus* moving slowly towards the open mouth of Aston Creek. 'That's not a Royal Navy ship. Looks like a merchant vessel to me. I don't know what they think they are doing there, but if they obstruct us we shall ram them,' he said to his bosun.

The *Saracen* was now gaining speed and heading for the open sea, but Josh was a very skilful captain and tactician. He had already anticipated Watson's thoughts. That was the reason he had ordered his ship to stand away from the mouth of the creek. He was fully aware that in a desperate bid to escape the full force of the law, the pirate captain would ram his way to freedom.

'Open the gun ports, and stand ready,' called Josh.

The *Saracen* was nearly into the open sea now. Watson's lieutenant saw the gun ports open. 'Captain, look, that ship is fully equipped with cannon.' His cry was trembling with fright.

'Get the gun ports open quickly,' answered Jacob Watson. The man went away, shouting orders as he ran.

Josh had again anticipated Watson's next move. 'Begin firing.'

The side of the *Pegasus* seemed to erupt as twelve cannons opened fire at the same time. From the headland it looked as though the ship was belching flame. Tom, James, Jonathan and Silas cheered.

The cannon salvo raked the *Saracen*. Parts of the ship's side disintegrated with the impact of cannonballs finding their target. Two balls went wide and landed harmlessly into the sea. A further cannonball hit the forward mast. It didn't break, but it was badly splintered and began creaking.

Within seconds Josh's men had reloaded and fired another round of twelve cannonballs. This time nine balls hit home into the *Saracen*'s side. Splintered timber was flailing some of the pirate crew with deadly effect. Gaping holes were now evident in the stricken ship.

The bosun decided he had had enough. 'Abandon ship. It's every man for himself!'

Jacob Watson was again purple with rage. 'So you have appointed yourself captain of the ship?'

'There isn't much of the ship left to be captain of,' was the terrified man's reply.

Jacob Watson drew his sabre with lightning speed and thrust it straight into his bosun's chest. 'If you want to be captain, try dying like a captain.'

The man fell to the deck, crying with the excruciating pain. He had a puzzled look on his contorted face. He had always been loyal to Watson, so why? That was his last thought.

The pirate crew had taken the call as official and began leaping overboard. Jacob Watson looked around him to see just two men left on board staring at him, awaiting an order. 'Don't just stand looking at me, get the small boat from the poop deck and haul it over the side. It's our only chance,' he barked.

Jonathan Smyth had been watching the spectacle from the hilltop and now realised that Watson was still planning to slip the net. He watched the small rowboat being lowered into the water and Watson lowering himself down the rope to join his two men in the boat. 'Come on, let's get down to the beach. The captain is still intent on escaping.' Tom, James and Silas followed their master down the steep incline towards the beach.

Josh ordered a longboat to be lowered to sail towards the sinking wreck of the *Saracen* and pick up the survivors. The trooper captain also had the same idea and directed his men to pick up the swimmers.

Jacob Watson believed he was outwitting his enemy by sailing away from his stricken ship from the opposite side to where the survivors were being picked up. He didn't know that Jonathan Smyth had observed his actions from the hilltop.

The first light of dawn was now creeping across the night sky. Jonathan and his three comrades reached the shingle beach and ran around the horseshoe-shaped cove to the side where Watson was expecting to land the small rowboat. Jacob Watson and his two men beached the boat and began hurrying towards the tree line.

'Not so fast,' called Smyth. Watson looked round in amazement.

'Who the blazes are you?'

'Your captor, and possibly the worst enemy you'll ever have.'

Watson and his two men drew their swords and stood to face Smyth and his men.

'You are not a soldier or a watchman, why are you my enemy? And I think I should know your name.'

'Very well, my name is Smyth, Jonathan Smyth. You became my enemy when you invaded the house of one of my dearest friends. You injured him badly and then set fire to his property. You and your men went on to terrorise villages and the people living in those villages, killing some before stealing their goods. Those people are people from the county where I was born and raised. Therefore you have as good as attacked me. For that, I intend to see you swinging from the gallows.'

Watson's eyes narrowed. His face took on an evil grimace. 'You will try. You should have stayed in your comfortable house and not interfered in my business. Your friend will be able to say you died at the hands of Jacob Watson.'

Watson lunged with his sword. Jonathan anticipated the move and sidestepped clear of the flashing blade.

Watson's two men took their captain's cue to begin battle. One of them struck out at Tom, who was nearest him. Tom saw the blade coming and parried it safely away. Silas didn't wait for the pirate near him to strike; he brought his sharp sabre across the man's chest. The man howled in pain as his chest opened up and blood spurted out. He fell to the ground, dying.

Smyth and Watson were now engaged in a full-scale sword fight. They were well-matched as they lunged and parried with each other. Silas wanted to help his master, but Jonathan shouted, 'No, Silas, I don't want him dead! I want him to face the hangman's noose.'

Tom and James had met their match with the remaining pirate, who was taking on both lads and holding his own successfully. Silas stepped up behind the pirate and struck him hard on the head with the handle of his sabre. The man dropped like a stone. 'Tie him up,' said Silas dryly. James had to smile at Silas's style.

'Tell me when you want a rest. You seem to be dragging this on a bit,' Silas sarcastically said to Jonathan.

Watson saw an opening in Smyth's defence and lunged forward. Jonathan reacted a bit late and sidestepped. The blade caught his jacket and rent it open. The impetus had carried Watson slightly past his opponent's body. Jonathan took advantage and brought the basket cage handle of his sword sharply down across Watson's head. Watson staggered forward with the impact. Silas saw his opportunity and hit the staggering pirate captain with a fearsome hammer blow to the man's chin. He dropped to the floor unconscious. 'Tie him up,' Silas ordered Tom and James.

'Why did you do that, Silas? I was getting the better of him.'

Silas grinned, 'I was getting bored.' Jonathan, Tom and James all guffawed with laughter. Silas sniggered and walked over to the little boat to see if anything of any use had been left in it.

Both the recovered prisoners were marched up to the hilltop to be corralled with the soaking wet pirates dragged from the sea and captured men from the hilltop battle. The Army officer looked very satisfied with his haul. He instructed his sergeant to load them onto two awaiting hay wagons that his runner had managed to commandeer. The pirates were securely lashed to each other and further tied to the carts, the sergeant making doubly sure that his prisoners were not going to escape him.

The *Pegasus* had anchored in the mouth of the creek, and some of the crew had rowed ashore in their longboat. Josh strolled up to his one-time captain. 'Hello, Captain, it's good to see you again.'

'It is really good to see you too, Josh, and my heartfelt thanks for rescuing us.' The two men hugged each other.

'Caleb told us about these villains. It was our privilege to help.'

The Army captain approached. 'I would feel it an honour if you would introduce me to your friend,' he asked Jonathan Smyth.

'Certainly, this is the captain of the *Pegasus*, Joshua Walker. Josh, this is Captain Alan Quartermaine.' The two men shook hands warmly.

'How do you know Mr Smyth, Josh?' asked the officer. Before Josh could answer, Jonathan butted in.

'Josh, Alan, I am going to have a word with some of the crew.' He strolled away.

Josh and Alan sat on a nearby rock. 'Mr Smyth used to be the owner of the *Pegasus*. We had some good times together. When he wanted to return to his land-based life, he gave the ship to all his crew.'

Alan looked staggered. 'That was a generous gesture.'

Josh was careful not to mention that, in his darker past, Jonathan had been a kind of pirate himself, albeit not the villainous type that Watson was. When

148

Josh had finished his tale, Quartermaine exclaimed, 'What a remarkable man Jonathan Smyth is, and generous to boot.'

Josh smiled. 'Yes, we love the man.'

Jonathan milled about between his old crew, patting them on the back and shaking hands. Caleb was among them. 'Come on, Caleb, you are going home with me,' he smiled. A wide beam spread across Caleb's face.

The Army captain walked across to Jonathan Smyth. 'When I have delivered these villains to the authorities, I shall recommend that you and your men and the crew of the *Pegasus* be honoured at a ceremony in Exeter. I hope you will receive the honour.' Josh asked his crew if they wanted to attend. A cheer went up.

Epilogue

On their way home to Credlington Manor, Jonathan Smyth and his comrades decided to stop off at Windfell Manor to check on Squire Brassington's recovery and tell him of the outcome of their adventure. Brassington was delighted that the pirates had been brought to justice. He thanked Jonathan and his friends for all they had done.

Back home life soon returned to normal for Tom, James and Jonathan Smyth. Tom told his friend James that life seemed a little dull after their latest escapade.

'Till next time,' responded James.

A month later, a messenger arrived at the manor. Jonathan received the edict to attend a ceremony in the great hall in Exeter, where he and his friends would be honoured on behalf of all the citizens of the county of Devon.

It was a very cold but sunny day when Smyth, Tom, James, Silas and Caleb arrived at the great hall at Exeter to be greeted by the whole crew of the *Pegasus*. Inside, a resplendent Captain Alan Quartermaine met them. It took a long time for everyone to shake hands with each other.

'Have the pirates been put on trial yet?' asked Jonathan.

'Yes, all were found guilty of murder, arson, robbery and violence. They are to meet the hangman next week.'

The ceremony was a lavish affair, and a wonderful day, enjoyed by everyone there. The night sky was rapidly overtaking the daylight when the friends bid their farewells to each other outside the hall.

'Another adventure completed,' said Jonathan to his old crewmates.

'Till you send for us again,' laughed Josh.

BOOK 3

Against the Outlaws

Chapter 1

The chilly spring morning was showing signs of promise as the sun began its climb upwards into the clear sky.

James Purdy was galloping across the long meadow heading away from Credlington Manor. His big chestnut mare seemed to be enjoying the morning canter.

Over the two years since his last adventure, James had become heavily involved in managing the livestock side of the day-to-day running of the huge estate. Jonathan Smyth quickly recognised that James really enjoyed all aspects of rearing and managing the estate's cattle, sheep and the horses belonging to the farm business that operated in the auspices of the Credlington Manor estates. Smyth encouraged James in his increasingly enthusiastic vocation. It was an ideal situation because he could trust James, who was honest to a fault and wouldn't tolerate any undue dealings.

Jonathan Smyth had now completed all the legal documents that would confirm Tom Bascombe and James Purdy as his legal heirs. He was pleased that both lads had accepted their responsibilities with such enthusiasm. Tom had become more interested in the whole management side of the estate and the banking business; at times Smyth began to think that Tom showed more flair than he ever did.

He had accompanied Tom on an occasion when he had visited one of the bank branches. Tom had scanned the day ledgers and discovered an anomaly in the bank's dealings. He quietly asked the manager for an explanation for the hardly recognisable error. The manager took the attitude 'How can a young man in his early twenties tell me what is wrong and what is right?' He didn't know that Jonathan Smyth had spent a lot of time and money educating Tom, because he realised that Tom had a very good brain and was a quick learner.

The manager responded in a haughty tone, 'The error is insignificant, and the bank will not suffer any financial loss.'

Tom looked at the man in disbelief. 'So that is all right then, in your opinion. My calculation tells me that a discrepancy of five guineas exists on this ledger.'

'That's as maybe, but as I have said, the bank is not the loser,' replied the manager.

At this point Tom was seething with anger. 'You are intimating that one of our customers is five guineas short in his balance and will not know about it. May I remind you that this bank has been more successful than other banks because we have always been trustworthy and scrupulously honest with all our customers? They rely on us, as most of our clients cannot read, write or add up money,' Jonathan Smyth stood to one side and watched, but said nothing.

The manager looked red-faced but did not reply.

'Well, where has the money gone?'

Still the man did not answer.

'I can only assume that you have stolen this money by deceit from one of our customers.' The man still failed to respond.

'Your continued silence convicts you of this crime.

You will wait outside the office while I discuss your future with Mr Smyth. I will send for you in a while.' With a wave of his hand Tom dismissed the man.

When the man had left the room, Tom asked Jonathan what he wished should be done with the manager.

'What can I add?' said Smyth.

'Well, it is your bank, and he is your employee,' responded Tom.

'You have made your mind up that he should be dismissed, haven't you?'

'Yes,' was Tom's terse reply.

'Well, you must stand by your convictions. You have basically accused the man of being dishonest, and I have to agree with you that the last thing a good bank needs is a crooked employee. My decision is that what you have started, you must finish. I may add that I think you are correct, this man is no good for our business.'

Tom called the man back into the small office.

'It is my opinion that you have besmirched this bank. By what you have declined to say I can only assume that you have robbed one of our customers, who relies on our honesty and integrity for his daily dealings, of five guineas. Have you anything to say in your defence?'

'I shall tell you nothing. You are nothing but an upstart. My employer is Mr Smyth, not you.'

Jonathan Smyth cut him short. 'Sir, how dare you speak to Tom Bascombe in this way. Tom is my representative in this and many other matters, most of which do not concern you. I totally agree with his thinking and reasoning, and by your reluctance to say what has transpired in your dealings with the money, I think that you have something to hide. This, together with the unforgivable outburst we have just seen, leaves me no alternative but to cease your employment with the bank.'

The man scowled at Smyth and Tom. 'Both of you will regret this.' He turned on his heel and slammed the door as he left.

Tom looked at Smyth. 'We shall have to reimburse the customer the five guineas. Oh, and I appreciate you standing up for me.'

Jonathan smiled. 'Your judgement was absolutely correct. The bank has to be grateful for your keen eye.'

Smyth called in the chief clerk, who in the past had acted as a deputy for the manager, and explained what had transpired. He further went on to ask if the man wanted to accept the role of being the manager. The man had a young family and the extra salary would come in very useful. He accepted with grateful thanks.

As Smyth and Tom stepped out into the street, Jonathan patted Tom on the shoulder. 'Let's go to the inn. I owe you a nice lunch.'

Later that afternoon, the two arrived back at the manor house. Jonathan strode into the big kitchen and asked the cook to prepare them a warm drink. The outer kitchen door opened from the stable yard. James came through, looking bright and breezy. 'Is there any bread and cheese? I am really hungry.'

Cook smiled at him. 'Are you having a late lunch, sir?'

Jonathan Smyth grinned, 'Bring his food into the great hall along with our drinks, please, Martha.'

'So what have you been busying yourself with today,

James?' he said as they walked down the passageway towards the big hall.

'We are getting some sheep and cattle ready to go to market later this week.'

'You are getting to be one of the best farm managers in the county. It is common knowledge among the top farmers,' said Smyth.

'Why, thank you for the compliment. I wouldn't put myself in such high esteem. I consider myself still learning.'

'We all learn till the day we die,' replied Smyth.

Chapter 2

The months seemed to fly by. Summer was approaching fast. The days were getting longer. The sun and warmer rains were nourishing the cereal and vegetable crops. James was delighted that his cattle were looking well-nourished on the very green grass they were constantly munching.

James hardly ever seemed to be in the house these days. After an early breakfast he was astride his horse and mustering his staff in their duties.

The two lads seemed to be like whirlwinds to Jonathan Smyth. He wondered if he ever had the enthusiasm and energy that these two young men possessed.

After the evening meal Jonathan sat by the open fireplace, smoking his clay pipe.

'James hasn't been home yet. I wonder what's keeping him out this late?'

Tom looked up from his reading. 'I haven't seen him since this morning. I will ask Johnson if he has been home.' Minutes later he was back. 'No one has seen him all day. Should we be worried yet?'

'Not yet. He may have some pressing business. He is liable to come and go at all hours.'

Five minutes later Jonathan looked towards Tom and said, 'I was in Burton Saint Mary earlier today. A couple of the townsfolk were telling me that some highway robbers had been causing havoc around the area. Apparently the mail coach was held up on Tuesday. I must tell Silas and Caleb that highwaymen are in the area. We need to remain diligent at all times and tell James when we see him. When you go out, always make sure you are well armed.' Tom acknowledged the warning.

The following morning, Tom came galloping down the main stairway and burst into the morning room where Smyth was sitting eating his breakfast.

'What on earth are you dashing about the place at this early hour for?'

'Jonathan, it's James. His bed hasn't been slept in.'

'Are you sure?'

'Well, I knocked on his door and there was no response, so I looked in. When he leaves his bed in the morning it looks as though he has been rounding up his precious cattle during the night. This morning, his bed is just as the maid left it yesterday, all crisp and tidy.'

Jonathan's brow furrowed in thought. 'I can't think where he could be. Go and find Silas and Caleb.'

Minutes later Tom was back with both of them and Jonathan told the two men of Tom's discovery. 'Did James go out with either of you two yesterday?'

Silas answered first. 'I only passed the time of day with him yesterday morning as he was preparing his horse.'

Caleb said, 'He was over with one of the farm workers in the north meadow about midday. I saw them as I was clearing some hedges out there. The last I saw of him, he was trotting off down towards the stream, which as you know is really low down from the meadow, so he disappeared from my view after that. That was the last I saw of him yesterday.'

'Would you find the man he was with and fetch him to me, please, Caleb.'

Caleb turned on his heel, and his heavy boots could be heard hurrying down the wooden flooring of the corridor.

Some time later he returned with a short stocky man, dressed in a rough woollen labourer's dark jacket. He had a red sweaty scarf about his neck. On entering the wood-panelled walled room, the man's eyes quickly took in surroundings that he probably had never seen before. On seeing Jonathan Smyth he hurriedly removed his hat in deference to his master.

'Can you tell us when you last saw Master Purdy yesterday, please.'

The man, not used to being in such surroundings and elite company, stuttered without a coherent word coming out.

'Take your time. There is no hurry,' reassured Smyth.

The labourer composed himself. 'Well, sir, I was a-working with Master Purdy sorting out some cattle for the beef market in the morning. I sits down to eat my meal under one of the trees, and he tells me he will see me a bit later on. He then rides towards the stream and I never sees him anymore. I thought it a bit odd, but I just got on with what he had told me to do, and come the evening, I went home. That's all I know, sir.'

Smyth thanked him and dismissed him.

Tom, Silas and Caleb had got used to Smyth's thinking moments and knew better than to disrupt him in mid-thought.

'Silas and Caleb, round up four of the best men we have. Take two each and search the area around the north meadow and the stream. If you find nothing, keep spreading out your search. Tom and I will ride into town and ask around. We shall all meet back here before dusk.'

Silas and Caleb gave their master the naval curled-finger salute touching their brows as they had always done when a distinct order had been made.

The sun was in the final stages, dipping beyond the horizon, as Smyth and Tom came clattering into the courtyard of the manor. They dismounted and strode into the house. Minutes later Silas and Caleb arrived.

Johnson the butler rapped loudly on the main hall door and entered.

'Sir, a letter was delivered while you were out.' He handed the carefully folded paper to Smyth, who opened it.

He read through the contents and then with an ashen face, asked Johnson, 'Did you see the person who delivered this?'

'Yes, sir, he was one of the young lads from the village. I thanked him and he went on his way.'

'What does it say?' asked Tom.

Jonathan Smyth just handed the letter to Tom. Tom read the contents out loud.

'We are holding one of your people, a man calling himself James. If you want to see him again alive, you will pay a ransom of 1,000 guineas to us. The money is to be left at the base of the signpost for Croxstead. You have two days to raise the money.'

Chapter 3

'What do we do now?' asked Tom.

'If we can't come up with knowing any more about the rogues who have kidnapped James, we'll have no alternative than to pay the ransom.'

Silas was furious. 'All the years me and Caleb have been with you, we have never caved in to threats such as this. I say we discover who these people are and teach them a lesson that puts the fear of the Almighty into them.'

Jonathan looked into Silas's eyes and calmly replied, 'I know how you feel. If I knew who these people are I would set off right now and take them off the face of the earth. The problem here is, they could carry out their threat and kill James. That is the last thing I wish to see.'

It was Tom who diffused the tense atmosphere. 'It occurs to me that by asking for such a large amount of money, they intend keeping James in good condition until they have got it. The danger period comes after they have been paid, there would be nothing to stop them from killing James. I think that we should get some form of rules here.'

'Rules? What kind of rules?' asked Jonathan.

'We need a handover arrangement. We agree to hand over the money in return for James being handed to us.'

Silas scratched his head. 'How do we contact them

to tell them the rules for this handover?'

Tom smiled, 'We'll begin by finding out the lad who brought the letter. Someone must have asked him to deliver it. Then we shall try and make contact with these rogues through that source. They can't think that we'd just leave a satchel of money by a road signpost. I hope the delay will help to keep James alive while we find out who these people are.'

Jonathan gave a little clap. 'That is wonderful reasoning, Tom. I am quite ashamed that my brain didn't come up with such good sense. What we need to agree on is a sound strategy. Ask Johnson to bring us some food.'

Tom said, 'I have had some further thoughts.'

Jonathan looked up. 'Oh, what?'

'I don't think you can get involved in our investigations.'

Jonathan looked astounded. 'Why on earth not?'

'Simply because you are too well known. Your asking round may jeopardise James's life. If any of the rogues discover that you are asking questions they may well kill James and move on.'

'I hadn't thought of that. You may be right. So what do you plan to do?'

'Silas and I will form one team. Caleb and Thomas from the stables will form the second team. We will scout round and arrange to meet up at a predetermined spot and see what we have found out.'

'Is Thomas trustworthy?'

Silas answered, 'Thomas is as good a man as you would find anywhere.'

The following morning Jonathan met Silas, Caleb and Thomas before they set off. Tom's scurrying feet heralded his tardiness as he emerged outside the kitchen doorway.

'Sorry I'm late. I had a job finding some really old clothes.'

Jonathan looked at him in disbelief.

Tom was dressed in an old ripped shirt, which had grimy stains down the front. The knees of his breeches were holed and dirty. His shoes had been scuffed to make them look really old. Traces of dirt had been applied to his cheeks.

'Good gracious, you look like a street urchin.'

'That's the idea,' replied Tom.

'You look more unkempt than Silas, Caleb and Thomas, and I thought they looked like tramps,' Jonathan grinned. He wished them luck as they trotted out of the stable yard.

At the crossroads Tom instructed Caleb and Thomas to find out as much information as possible around the area of Croxstead. 'Ask around. See what you can discover about the lad who may have delivered the letter or the people behind the letter. Anything you can glean. Meet back here at sunset.'

Silas and Tom set off for Burton Saint Mary. Arriving in the town, the pair rode up to the town stables and left their horses in the care of the ostler. Minutes later they were walking down the main street. They entered the Green Man Inn and ordered ale.

'We be looking for a young'un who delivered a letter yesterday to a house round hereabouts,' said Silas to the innkeeper.

The man looked puzzled. 'I can't help you. Try one of the locals over in the corner.'

Silas made his way to a group of farm workers.

'Morning gents, I'm trying to find a youth who sometimes delivers letters.'

The men looked at each other. Eventually one of the group said, 'The only two as I know is Simon, whose father works at Topps Farm, or Jack Hobson. He lives at the last cottage on Gray Street.'

Silas thanked them and emptied his tankard, and Tom and he left the inn.

'Jack Hobson is the nearest, so we'll try there first.'

Not long after, Silas was tapping loudly on a very weathered door. A middle-aged woman opened the door. She had an old blue dress on covered by a white apron.

'Good day, madam, can I talk to Jack?'

'He is in the back. I'll shout him.'

A tall, skinny lad of fifteen came to the door.

'I'm told you deliver letters for folks from time to time?'

'Yes, do you want one taking somewhere?'

'No, what I want to know is did you deliver a letter to Credlington Manor yesterday?'

The lad looked suspiciously at Silas and Tom.

'There's money in it for you if you did,' said Silas.

The lad's eyes brightened up. 'I wish it was me. We could use the money.'

Tom took pity on him and put a few coppers into his hand. 'Thanks for your honesty. Do you know anybody who could have taken the letter?'

'Could have been Simon up at Topps Farm.' He thanked them for the cash and directed them to the farm.

It was a two-mile trudge. Eventually they found the lad they were looking for. After a similar set of questions he confessed he was the one Silas and Tom were seeking.

Tom waved a handful of coins in front of the boy. 'Who asked you to deliver the letter?'

The boy hopefully put his hand out for the money. Tom clenched his fist. 'When we have an answer.'

'This man was coming out of the Royal Oak and I was standing outside. He offered me a half guinea if I would go straight up to the Manor. At first I thought it would be nightfall before I got back home, but for half a guinea it didn't matter. My dad don't get that much in a week at the farm.'

'So describe this man. Better still, do you know his name or where he lives?'

The lad, now eager to get the money, responded gladly. 'I heard the men with him call him Jake. He is not quite as tall as you. Thinner and dressed like both of you. Oh, and he has sandy hair with a ponytail. Can't tell you where he hails from.'

Tom opened his hand and the boy gratefully took the coins.

Walking back towards the town, Tom told Silas of his plan.

'I need to try and get myself in with this gang.'

Silas nearly exploded. 'What? If they found out they would kill you. More to the point, Jonathan would never allow it.'

'Jonathan will never find out. You will hover in the background to keep a watch on me. Tonight when we meet Caleb we'll tell him. He and Thomas will be our go-between.'

'I can't say I like the idea,' said Silas.

'It may be the only way to save James. Furthermore, I am trusting you and Caleb to keep this a secret.'

Silas stroked his chin. 'You know how to push loyalty to the limit.'

Chapter 4

The following morning Silas and Tom slipped out of Credlington Manor's kitchen door as dawn was breaking.

Tom had taken care to leave a note on the breakfast table for Jonathan to see. Its simple message was that he and Silas had left early to continue their investigations.

Out on the road Tom removed the scarf wrapped around his head. It was a bright sunny morning, and he didn't want anything on his head.

'Good God! What have you done to yourself?' exclaimed Silas.

'I shaved my head to make me look more menacing.'

'It certainly does that.'

Tom was dressed similar to the previous day, with shabby, torn clothing and smears of dirt on his face and arms. Silas thought he looked as though he had been on the run for weeks.

'Are you armed?'

Tom smiled, 'I have a sheathed dagger down my boot. I can't risk having a pistol. It would look too blatant.'

'Don't worry, I have pistols in the saddle panniers,' replied Silas.

The pair rode into Burton Saint Mary and made their way to the town stables where they had arranged to meet Simon, who was to point out to them who had given him the letter to deliver.

The trio ambled up and down various streets, trying not to look too suspicious. Eventually Simon's face brightened up. 'That's one of them on that corner.'

'Is that the man who gave you the letter?' asked Tom.

'No, but he was with the man. They seemed to be friends.'

Tom and Silas thanked Simon and told him to go about his business.

'Right, I am going to follow him. Try and stay away from me, but close enough if I need you.'

Silas nodded his agreement and wished him luck. Tom slipped across the road to trail behind the man. Minutes later the man entered the Green Man Inn. Tom followed, leaving a decent time gap.

The room was already fairly well occupied. Most were farmers who had brought goods to the market and were meeting friends they only saw on market days. Pipe smoke drifted round the room. Men chattered and laughed.

Tom quickly looked round the room. He saw the man he had been following, who was sitting with another man, ginger-haired with a ponytail.

Tom made his way to the bar and ordered a tankard of ale. He glanced round to see Silas hovering near the doorway. Tom weaved his way between the customers towards the two seated men. When he was behind the man with the ponytail, he tipped his tankard slightly. The ale dribbled down the ginger-haired man's shirt.

'Oi! What do you think you're doing?'

He looked round to see the tall, broad-shouldered, scruffy-looking individual who had spilt his drink on him.

Tom looked surprised. 'Oh, I am sorry, somebody nudged my arm. Can I buy you a drink?'

The pony-tailed man looked Tom up and down. 'And where might you get the money together to buy anyone a drink?'

'You'd be surprised where I can get money. Do you want a drink or not?'

The ginger-haired man said, 'Thanks, if you care to buy me a drink, I'll accept.'

Tom went to the bar and bought two tankards of ale. He placed them on the table in front of the two men. 'Even I have manners. I couldn't get you one without your friend.'

'Thanks, come and sit with us.'

Tom offered his hand, 'I am Gil Archer.'

Both men shook hands in turn.

'I am John Simmons, and this is Charlie Blake.'

Tom thought that wasn't bad going: five minutes and he was sharing drinks with them. He now knew that the ginger-haired man was John Simmons.

'So you reckon you can get money when you need it, eh?' said Blake. 'Tell us what your source is.'

'I haven't known you long enough to tell you my secrets,' responded Tom.

Blake looked cross at Tom's answer. 'All right, let's get to know each other better. We are always on the search for funds. We are not poor farmers. We like to think we can do better than to struggle behind a plough for a pittance.'

'So how do you make a living?' asked Tom.

Simmons paused. 'Well, let's say if somebody seems to be troubled with a surplus of money, we help them out.' He and Blake laughed.

'You mean you rob people,' whispered Tom. The two men looked shocked. Tom broke the icy atmosphere. 'You are in the same business as me, then.'

The two men looked at each other, and then a grin spread across their faces.

'You don't look as though you are very successful,' said Simmons.

Tom grinned, 'These are my working clothes.'

The men laughed out loud at Tom's quick response.

'You don't seem a bad sort. Why not join forces with us?'

'I could use some help at times.'

Again Blake and Simmons laughed out loud. 'I like your sense of humour,' said Blake.

After a few more drinks the three left the inn. Tom raised his eyebrows at Silas as he brushed past him.

'So where do you ply your trade? I use the term trade loosely, of course.'

Again Blake and Simmons chuckled at Tom's humour.

'Well, it's not just us two. There are others in it. We carry out the business and throw our spoils into the pot and then share the loot out equally. That way everyone of us either gets a good share or a poor share according to how successful we've been.'

'I suppose it relies on honour among thieves,' grinned Tom.

Charlie Blake laughed again. 'If you are no good at robbing, you certainly are witty.'

'I'm not sure I want to be part of a large gang. I always work alone.'

Blake butted into the conversation. 'Oh, don't worry, there are just six of us. Most of us have known each other for years, and recently a man talked us into joining forces to form a group and cover a bigger area. He seems to know what he is about. He is very clever with sums. This suits us, as most of us can't

172

read or write, let alone add numbers together. So someone to organise us and share out the spoils is great.'

'Who is this great man?'

Simmons quickly interrupted before his partner could answer. 'I don't think we can tell you his name.'

'Why the secrecy?'

'Wait till everyone gets to know you better. When you are trusted you will get to know him.'

'Where are you living?' Blake asked Tom.

'Some months ago, I came across an old disused barn. Nobody seems to lay claim to it, so there I stay.' Tom cast his eye towards the sky. 'Looks like rain coming. I think I'll be heading home.'

'Shall we see you tomorrow, Gil?'

'Yes, see you near the inn, mid-morning.'

Chapter 5

Wandering out of the town Tom was left wondering what his next plan should be. He was now trying to live a life of lying and intrigue. Could he keep up the pretence and find James?

'Tom!' A hushed voice was calling his name. Tom looked round but couldn't see anyone. 'Over here.' Tom moved away from the road towards the trees skirting the highway. Again the hushed voice. 'Tom!' A beckoning hand now became visible from behind a large tree. Tom moved towards it and ventured cautiously around the tree.

'Silas!'

Silas's grinning face was more than comforting to Tom.

'I've been following you most of the time. When you talked near the stocks I had no cover, so I made my way here and waited for you.'

Tom told Silas all that had occurred during the conversation with the two men and of his new assumed name of Gil Archer.

'I met Caleb this afternoon. I'm afraid Mr Smyth suspected that something was going on. He forced Caleb to tell him the truth. He's far from pleased. He told Caleb that he was preparing to pay the ransom for James and that would have been an end to the matter. Caleb talked him round a bit and explained that it was possible they would take the money and still harm James so he couldn't identify his kidnappers. Mr Smyth agreed and is sending a messenger to the meeting point to ask for more time to raise such a large sum. He hopes that will give us more time to find out where James is being kept.'

'That means I have to work harder at getting in with them,' said Tom. 'I suspect they'll expect me to prove myself before they take me into their confidence. Possibly rob somebody. How I do that I have no idea.'

Silas was quiet for a moment. 'I have an idea,' he said. 'Maybe I can arrange with Mr Smyth to ask Squire Brassington if he would let you rob him. Only fake an injury, mind. You could prove yourself to them that way.'

Silas mounted his horse and headed back to the Manor, leaving Tom to find himself a place to sleep for the night.

Tom spent an uncomfortable night, managing only snatches of sleep under an overhanging rock outcrop in the forest.

He awoke to find a drizzle of rain in the air. Some blue sky was evident, so the morning would hopefully improve. He gathered his few belongings together and washed in a nearby stream before setting off to town.

He ate a simple breakfast at the Green Man Inn, and then waited to see if his acquaintances from yesterday would show up.

An hour later Charlie Blake walked into the inn parlour. 'Morning, Charlie, you on your own today?'

Blake waved Tom towards him and led him out onto the street. They walked without a word to the end of the street. Blake ushered Tom to the rear of the town stables. Three other men were squatting against the wall of the building.

Tom looked them over on his approach. One was a little below medium height; his hair looked unkempt, his clothing grey and drab. The other bore a striking resemblance to Charlie Blake, except that he was taller and more skeletal. The third man in the group was John Simmons.

Tom decided to be flippant. 'Is this the whole gang, then?'

Simmons sneered, 'You ain't been with us long enough to know all about us yet.'

Blake quickly diffused the obvious rancour that Simmons seemed to have against Tom.

'This is my twin brother, Freddy, and this is Alan Grey.'

'You told me yesterday there were six of you?'

Simmons quickly jumped in again, 'You ask too many questions for my liking.'

Tom apologised.

Charlie Blake sensed Simmons's uneasiness. 'The other two are working on another job. That's why they are not here.'

Simmons pushed his way in front to face Tom. 'We had a talk about you last night. You'll have to prove your worth before you can join us. You'll want to put in some money or something of value as your share for joining. One of us will go with you to find out how good you are.'

Tom decided that just lying down and letting Simmons walk all over him would make him more of a target for Simmons' suspicions and then bullying.

'Let's get something straight from the start. I'm not desperate to join up with you lot. I can make my own way without any of you,' he said, glaring at Simmons.

Simmons was taken aback by Tom's reaction. He

suddenly realised that Tom was taller and more powerfully built than him. He hadn't noticed this before.

'So what do you want me to do to prove myself?'

Blake quickly answered Tom's question. He could see that Simmons was antagonising Tom. 'You could rob some rich landowner and bring the spoils to share between us all. You included, of course.'

'Is that all?' answered Tom, derisively.

Simmons sneered, 'One of us comes with you to watch you.'

Tom shrugged his shoulders, 'That's fine by me as long as he doesn't get in my way. If I'm expected to do this, I'd better get going.' He turned on his heel and began walking away. 'See one of you here tomorrow.'

Blake jumped in, 'I'll meet you, Gil.'

Tom signalled his approval and marched off.

Chapter 6

In a disused big old hay barn some ten miles north of Burton Saint Mary, James was attempting to stretch himself against his bindings.

'What are you up to?' asked his guard as he heard James shuffling against the straw-covered floor.

'I have cramp. I need to stand for a while.'

The guard shuffled off through the narrow opening in the separating wall between the two sections of the building. A short while later he returned with a tall figure dressed in a long black riding coat and black boots. He wore a tricorn hat and a dark scarf covering most of the lower part of his face.

'Help him to stand up. Take the ropes from his ankles and let him walk about a bit. He is very valuable to us.' He spoke to James, 'Your master has agreed to pay the ransom. Your hands will remain bound and my colleague will re-tie your legs after your circulation has improved.'

'Thank you,' answered James.

As the man started back through the opening he turned to the other man. 'If he tries to escape, put a ball through his leg.'

Tom met Silas on the outside of town at the appointed meeting place.

'You haven't been followed. I watched you for the last two miles,' said Silas.

Tom flopped down against a big tree and told Silas what he had to do to prove himself.

'When you see Jonathan later today, ask him if he can arrange with Squire Brassington to let me rob him. To make it realistic I would need to break in somewhere, say an old side door. If you can arrange it today, meet me here tomorrow and let me know.'

'Consider it done, Tom.' Silas mounted his horse and rode off towards the Manor.

Wandering back towards their hideaway, the four outlaws talked. 'There's something about Gil Archer I don't like,' said Simmons.

'I think we've got that message, including Archer,' responded Charlie Blake. 'Anyhow, you don't need to come tomorrow. I'll see how he performs. If you were around you'd help the people being robbed to bring Archer in front of the hangman and collect the reward.' Simmons laughed at the thought.

Tom woke up to see wispy clouds gliding across the early morning sky. At least it was a dry morning. He washed himself in the nearby stream, dried himself and set off to meet Silas.

'I thought you would appreciate some breakfast,' said Silas.

Tom tucked into the food whilst Silas told him about the plan for robbing the squire.

'Mr Smyth is giving the Squire a small amount of money for you to steal. Squire Brassington suggests you fake a hit over Robinson the butler's head and

179

they'll cover part of his head with sheep's blood to make it realistic. He will stagger out after you but fall down so you get away easily.'

'That's a good scheme. All that remains is for me to pick up my observer and get over to the Squire's place.'

'I'll stay in the background. Good luck, Tom.'

Tom made his way to the rear of the town stables and squatted on the ground, waiting for Charlie Blake to show up. Twenty minutes later Blake poked his head cautiously round the corner of the building. He saw Tom sat there on his own and walked towards him.

'Morning, Gil, it looks a good day for it.'

Tom shrugged his shoulders. 'What's the day got to do with it? If it was rainy we would get wet.'

'Where are we off to?'

'Last night I spotted a manor house and had a sneak round it when it had gone dark. It seems easy enough. It is about five miles from here, so I suggest we get started.'

'What? You intend to rob the place in broad daylight?'

'I thought you wanted to find out how good I am. If I robbed them at night it would be too easy and you wouldn't see as much.'

Blake smiled, 'You have plenty of guts, Gil. Let's be off, then.'

Just over an hour later the two men approached Squire Brassington's manor house. Tom pulled Blake into the cover of the trees. 'Stay here where you can see into the courtyard, but keep under cover in the undergrowth. Last night I noticed an old door on the far left. That is where I intend going in.'

Blake nodded his acceptance and laid himself into the foliage.

Tom skirted the house perimeter and scaled the wall onto the single-storey outbuildings near the side door. He dropped down into the small yard area where he knew that Blake couldn't possibly see him, and whistled softly.

Robinson poked his head round the slightly open door and waved to Tom that access was clear. Tom sprinted the few steps across the yard and made a fake but meaningful show of breaking into the building. He was now again out of Blake's eyesight.

'Good morning, Tom,' said Squire Brassington. 'Don't hurt Robinson.'

'You may do more damage covering him in animal blood,' chuckled Tom.

He let a minute or two lapse before he instructed Robinson to begin shouting and banging some metal pans together. The cook smeared blood on Robinson's head, Tom took the leather moneybag, and the shouting and banging began. Tom stumbled out of the back door with Robinson following him. Tom took a fake swipe at the butler's body. He staggered and fell to the ground. Tom ran as fast as he could out of the yard and into the nearby woods.

Half an hour later and two miles away from the Manor, Tom sat waiting under the cover of the trees. Blake approached from behind Tom. He saw he was alone and came up to him.

'Are you all right? Did you get hurt?'

'Of course I'm all right. It's that stupid old man who tried to stop me that may not be.'

'Yes, I saw the old man. He was covered in blood and then he tried to stop you until you hit him. How did he get that wound?'

181

Tom suspected that Blake was collecting the information to give his pals a verbal report. 'I went down a corridor without anybody spotting me and came to a doorway. I listened at the door and heard nothing. I opened the door and entered. There was a large dresser against a wall. I opened one or two of the drawers until I came across this moneybag. Then the man looked round the door and saw me. He came at me and I picked up a metal dish and hit him with it. That's when all the uproar started, so I made my exit as quick as I could. The rest you saw.'

Blake looked in the bag and grinned. 'You're a cool one.'

As Blake squatted down facing Tom, over his shoulder Tom caught sight of the edge of a black cloak protruding from behind a large tree. He smiled to himself, knowing it was Silas keeping an eye on him.

'Get yourself up, Gil, we have to meet the rest of the boys.' The two began the long walk back to Burton Saint Mary.

Some time later Blake and Tom stepped inside the Green Man Inn. They edged their way over to one of the corners, where Simmons, Freddy Blake and Alan Grey were sitting chatting.

'Well?' Simmons greeted them. 'Has Archer done the deed, or ran away scared?' he sneered.

Blake put his hand up to indicate that he would appreciate quiet while he recounted the tale. 'You wouldn't be so quick to condemn, if you had seen Gil in action. In broad daylight he managed to get into this 'ere big house, scouted through some rooms and found a bag of guineas. A man heard him and tried to restrain him. Old Gil here hit him with a pewter plate so hard that the man's head was covered in blood.'

Simmons interrupted, 'How do you know all this? Did you go in with him?'

'No, but I sees this man chase him from the house, and his head was covered in blood. Gil hit him again in the yard. This time he must have hit him that hard that the man stayed down on the ground. I tell you, John, you couldn't have done any better.'

Simmons sat back in his chair and chose not to comment.

Tom couldn't help thinking that his infamous deed being related in such glowing terms by Blake was making Simmons an even more dangerous enemy. He suspected that Simmons would be suffering from his hero of the hour crown being taken away from him and handed to Gil Archer. From now on he would be even more careful.

The coins were counted and placed back in the leather bag.

'So is Gil now one of us?' asked Freddy Blake.

'I think he is. What about the rest of you?' replied Charlie.

'He has my blessing,' said Freddy.

'Mine too,' chipped in Alan Grey.

'What about you?' Blake asked Simmons.

'I have to say yes.'

All but Simmons patted Tom on the back. From deep in one of the inn's dark corners Silas watched Tom's induction into the bunch of outlaws. Tom sighed with relief, unseen by his new comrades in crime.

'Does this mean I will have somewhere decent to sleep tonight?' Tom asked of his comrades.

Simmons broke in before anyone could speak. 'Don't

be in such a rush, Archer. We have another job to do before we sleep.'

'Can you ride a horse?' Charlie Blake asked.

'Of course I can, but I haven't got one. Why do I need a horse?'

Simmons summoned them closer together so that eavesdroppers couldn't overhear. 'The mail coach will be making its way to Exeter today. Its route takes it on the highway five miles west of here. It should pass there round about five o'clock. I've been surveying the area for a while now and discovered a great spot to lay in wait. We lay a trap for the coach, hold it up and steal the goods.'

The two Blakes and Grey grinned. 'Should go like a dream.'

'What about weapons? I haven't got any.'

'Don't worry, we are off to get fixed up with horses and weapons now,' whispered Charlie Blake.

Minutes later the five made their way out of the inn and along the main street towards the stables.

Chapter 7

The robbers made their way out of town via the back streets so as not to attract suspicion. Out on the main highway they broke their mounts into a trot. Tom suspected that the man managing the town stables was more crooked than honest. Like magic he had produced horses, pistols and black riding coats for all of them, all with winks, smiles and a nod of the head.

Silas watched from a distance as the small band made their way out of town. He decided that he should report back to Jonathan Smyth, as if he followed them he would definitely be seen out on the open road. He wheeled his horse round and headed back for the Manor house.

Back at Credlington Manor, Silas dismounted and stabled his horse. Jonathan had heard him arrive and went out to meet him. 'Give me the latest news, Silas.'

Silas told him all he had seen that day and told him of his decision not to follow the robbers. Jonathan nodded his approval.

'The worrying thing is that we don't know why they have equipped Tom with a horse, weapons and riding gear, and have all ridden off together.'

'I think they're planning a crime, but what?' replied Jonathan.

'You know, Silas, I have been really worried about poor James. We don't know whether he is all right or if they have harmed him. I have come to the decision that I should pay the ransom and get him home safely.'

Silas winced. 'Don't you think we should try and find out where James is being held first? These people could well take the ransom and still kill James so that he has no chance of identifying them.'

Jonathan pondered on Silas's words. 'You could well be right. Truth is, I honestly don't know what to do for the best.' They made their way back into the big house.

Tom was trailing behind the other four riders. Charlie Blake was riding just a few steps in the rear. Tom spurred his mount to catch up with Charlie.

'If we get separated, where do we meet up afterwards?'

Blake looked at Tom with suspicion. 'Why should we get split up?'

'Well, what if the mail coach is full of men armed to the teeth and a shooting match occurs? I would expect everybody to try and save themselves.'

Blake mulled over Tom's scenario for a few moments. 'I hadn't considered that. You may have a point. We use a disused barn, which is about five miles north of Moreton Bishop. You get to the Kings Arms and turn left on to a track that is overgrown in places. The barn is about half a mile down that track.'

Tom nodded his appreciation. He was hoping that Blake had just told him where his friend James was being held captive.

Half an hour later the gang drew their horses to a standstill.

'Right, get yourselves hidden in the wood, but make

sure you can see me give a signal and that you can see the highway. If we are spotted they will be alerted and take defensive action,' shouted Simmons.

They didn't have long to wait. In the distance came the clattering noise of horses' hooves and the rumble of metal-rimmed wheels.

Simmons lifted his arm in the air. When his arm dropped they would ride out onto the road and surround the mail coach. Surprise was the key to a successful operation.

The coach was now within a hundred yards of their hiding place. John Simmons's arm dropped. The five men burst out onto the road. Two quickly went to the rear. Simmons, Blake and his brother stopped their horses directly in front of the slow-moving coach, their long-barrelled pistols pointed directly at the coach driver and the assistant at his side. The man riding beside the driver was cradling a flintlock long-barrelled gun.

'Drop the weapon and hands in the air,' commanded Simmons.

Alan Grey signalled to Tom to look inside the coach while he kept him covered at a discreet distance. 'Keep your pistol at the ready, and be careful, Gil.' Tom nodded and headed for the right-hand door.

'Hands above your heads,' he ordered as he opened the door.

The door slammed into his body, which took Tom by surprise. He fell backwards. A tall, heavy-built man bounded from inside the coach and followed up his attack by leaping on Tom. Tom had seen the lumbering man's onslaught and rolled out of the way as the man hit the ground. Before the surprise had dawned on the attacker, Tom brought the heavy pistol down on the man's head. Tom jumped to his feet and brought his boot into the man's side before he could recover from the crack on his head. The man lay prone on the ground.

'I couldn't shoot, Gil, I might have hit you.'

'It's all right, I'm not hurt.'

At the front end of the coach, Simmons and his two colleagues had rendered the driver and assistant helpless and were now busy removing a box from beneath the driver's seat. Tom again approached the door to the inside of the vehicle. Three terrified-looking passengers stared out at him, one a middle-aged lady with a man of a similar age beside her. He was dressed in a heavy dark-blue coat, breeches and black calf-length boots. The lady was clad in a heavyweight printed dress and an overcoat and large hat. On the other seat sat a young lady who Tom guessed was a similar age to him. She also had a long travelling coat, and a bonnet covering her light brown hair.

'Please don't hurt us,' cried the older woman.

'Just get out of the coach,' called Alan Grey from astride his horse.

The occupants obliged. Meanwhile round at the front end of the coach Simmons was getting very frustrated with the driver. 'Give me the key to the strong box or I shall put a shot through your leg.'

The driver pleaded with Simmons, 'Sir, you should know that there isn't any mail driver who has a key to the mail strong box. It is opened at its destination by the mail supervisor.'

Simmons lifted his musket to the firing position. 'Hold it,' cried Charlie Blake. 'He's right. They don't trust the drivers with keys because of people like us.'

'We'll just have to break it open, then.'

Simmons put down his gun and took out his dagger.

He tried to slide the point of the weapon up into the closed lid. He managed to get the point just about half an inch between the lid and the body of the steel box. He hit the handle of the knife with the heel of his hand. The knife refused to penetrate any further.

Simmons was now extremely angry and began cursing and swearing at the obstinate box. He threw the dagger down onto the ground and picked up the musket. He held the gun by the barrel and swung the butt at the edge of the lid in an attempt to jar it open. Nothing moved. He swung the gun again in a vicious upward swing. The butt of the gun fractured. The wooden stock cracked loudly. He threw the damaged weapon to the ground and shouted loudly. Wondering what on earth was happening, Alan Grey jumped from his horse and ran to the front to find out what the unearthly noise was about.

Tom saw his opportunity. He knew that all the passengers would be robbed of any belongings they had. He grabbed the young girl's arm and pulled her towards the trees. As she was about to object he put his finger to his lips in a shush sign. 'Trust me, escape now. Run into the forest, and I will try and get back for you later. I am not one of these robbers, but I can't explain now. Go quickly.' The girl picked up the hem of her dress and ran off into the dense wood.

Luckily for Tom the other two passengers had not noticed his rapid action. They had been concentrating on the rage happening at the front end of the coach.

'Where has Anne gone?' said the older lady. Her husband just shrugged his shoulders.

The two Blakes, Simmons and Grey were now loudly arguing about how to open the steel box. 'Strap it onto one of the horses and take it with us,' suggested Charlie Blake.

'It may not be worth carting. That's why I wanted to open it,' answered Simmons.

The man that Tom had knocked unconscious had recovered and was now on the opposite side of the coach, hiding partly behind the rear horse of the four-horse team pulling the big coach. He had a pistol pointed at the gang. He fired and hit Alan Grey in the shoulder. Grey spun round, screaming in pain. The explosion scared the four horses and they lurched forwards pulling the vehicle down the road. The robbers scattered to each side of the highway.

Tom quickly realised that all this could go horribly wrong for his plan. He leaped onto the nearest horse and galloped off after the runaway coach.

Half a mile down the road he drew alongside the leading pair of horses. He knew that the only way to stop the panicking animals was to get on one of their backs and rein them in. The problem was he had never done this and was scared of falling between the horses. He stood up in the stirrups and attempted to stand on his own horse's back. He slipped and fell back into the saddle. In the near distance he could see a rise in the road as the highway began to climb a small hill. The horses would slow down on the hill. This had to be his only chance. A few yards up the hill the horses began to slow down. He steadied his own mount, climbed again in the saddle and leapt. He landed on his belly across the nearest horse's back. He gripped the harness and held on for dear life. Gradually he regained his balance and pulled himself into a sitting position on the animal. He hauled on the harness, gradually bringing the coach and horses to a stop.

He sat with sweat pouring down his face, offering comforting words to the snorting horses. After a while he composed himself. He tied his horse to the rear of the mail coach and hauled himself onto the driving platform. He turned the whole unit around and put the horses into a steady trot back to where his gang were relieving the passengers of their belongings.

Charlie Blake greeted him. 'How did you manage to stop that lot?'

'A lot of luck and stupidity,' replied Tom.

'We didn't need the coach, you could have let it go,' bawled Simmons.

'And when we have gone how, do you suppose these folks are to get to their destination?' said Tom, losing his temper with Simmons.

'The trouble with you, Archer, is you are a weak link in our organisation. I couldn't care less what happens to this lot.' Tom turned his back on Simmons and glanced round, looking for the young woman. She wasn't there. Hopefully she had done as Tom instructed and ran deep into the forest. The remaining passengers had now been stripped of their valuables. The middle-aged woman was sobbing. The man with her stood with his arm round her shoulder, comforting her.

The strong box was now lying on the ground with the lid open. 'So, how did you get the box open?' asked Tom.

'No thanks to John Simmons,' whispered Alan Grey. 'Charlie shot at the lock and then it was fairly easy to break off.'

'Anything of value in it?'

'A few gold pieces, a few guineas and some documents. Charlie put the lot in his saddlebag.

Our leader will sort it out when we get back to base.'

Tom wondered who this mystery leader was but it would cause further suspicion if he asked about him. For the time being he would keep his thoughts to himself.

The group mounted their horses and galloped away, leaving the driver and assistant of the coach gathering what was left of their belongings together and urging their passengers back into the coach.

Some time later the band of robbers approached a turnpike. Tom halted his mount. Charlie Blake also brought his horse to rein. 'What's the matter, Gil?'

'If I am going back with you, I need to collect my bits from my hideout. You told me where you are based, so I should be there before nightfall.'

Blake looked a little perturbed, but didn't object.

Chapter 8

Tom rode at a trot along the highway away from the four men and turned back to see them disappear in the distance. He wheeled his horse round and headed back towards where the hold-up had taken place. He tied his horse to a tree and hurried through the wood, calling out as he went. 'Lady, lady, lady.' He noticed the edge of her dark green coat protruding from the side of a large tree trunk. She was hiding as best she could behind the tree.

'I told you I would come back for you.'

'I don't understand. You are one of the robbers. I think you want to harm me.'

'Believe me, I don't want to harm you. That is why I told you to run and escape. I am going to find a farmhouse or a cottage to see if they will give you refuge.'

He led the suspicious young woman back to his horse and helped her to climb onto its back. Back on the road he explained why he was involved with the outlaws. He stressed that saving his friend James's life was his first priority.

'My name is Tom Bascombe.'

The girl seemed to relax. 'My name is Anne Berry. I live in Exeter with my parents. I have been visiting my aunt, who lives near London.'

Twenty minutes later Tom saw a small cluster of houses. He urged his horse towards the little community. He picked out the biggest house and rapped smartly on the door. An elderly man answered the door. Tom explained that there had been a hold-up of the Exeter stage and he had found this lady at the roadside in a distraught state. Would they be kind enough to shelter her till she could find her way back home? The man's wife appeared in the doorway. Tom repeated the story.

The ruddy-faced woman smiled broadly at the girl. 'Come inside, my dear. What a terrible ordeal. My husband has to take some produce to Exeter one day this week. He could go tomorrow.' The man nodded.

'I think this young woman should thank her lucky stars that such a honourable young man like you should happen to come along and rescue her,' smiled the ruddy-faced woman.

Anne lingered in the doorway after thanking the couple for their hospitality.

'Will you tell me where you live?' asked Tom.

She smiled and gave her address. Tom promised he would contact her again. He turned on his heel and mounted his horse for the long ride back to Moreton Bishop.

Darkness had taken over as Tom arrived in the community of Moreton Bishop. He headed on till he saw the Kings Arms, found the track and made his way carefully along it. Eventually he saw the stone-built barn in the distance. He tied his horse to a nearby tree and crept through the undergrowth for the remaining dozen or so yards, not wishing to walk into a trap that could have been laid for intruders. He was also aware that some of the band didn't trust him. He quietly crept round the outer edge of the building, all the time watching where he was treading.

Talking and the occasional laughter were emanating from inside. He could also see a dim light coming out of the chinks in the old stonework. Tom paused, wondering whether to walk inside. After moments of deliberation, he decided they would become even more suspicious if he didn't show up. He went back for his horse and led it to where the other horses were tethered. He removed the saddle and pulled out his sleeping blanket and entered the barn.

'We thought you had got lost,' sneered Simmons.

Tom ignored him. 'Do I just find a spot to bed myself down, or will I be taking somebody else's place?'

Charlie Blake answered. 'Over in the corner will be all right. There is some stew if you want some.'

'Thanks, I am really hungry.'

After he had finished his rude meal, Tom decided to find out some more information.

'So, this is your headquarters?'

'Not good enough for you, then?' said Simmons.

'No, it's fine for me. I have never been used to much. I just thought it is not very grand for you,' he replied, staring at Simmons.

An angry grimace appeared on Simmons's face. He rose to his feet. 'There is something about you I don't like.'

'It would be impossible if we liked everybody we meet in life. I can't honestly say I like you either.'

Simmons leaped the few steps to where Tom was squatting. Quick as a flash, Tom reacted and rolled away from the attack. Simmons tripped on a projection in the floor and fell heavily against the stone wall. Tom, now standing with his back to the wall, waited.

till the enraged Simmons rose to his feet, and again came at Tom.

Simmons lashed out towards Tom's head. Tom sidestepped and the man's fist hit the wall. He howled with pain. Tom struck Simmons on the side of his jaw, felling the man. Simmons sat on the floor, deciding whether he should continue the brawl. His fist hurt, as well as his jaw. Most of all, his pride had been crushed.

Tom realised he had to offer the man a face-saving way out. 'Is this really necessary? We've had a successful day. Nobody got hurt too badly, robbing the coach, and we came away better off than we started. The last thing I want to do is have a fight with any of you.'

Charlie Blake broke the atmosphere. 'Gil is right, we shouldn't be fighting amongst ourselves. Come on, John, stand up and shake hands with Gil.'

Simmons reluctantly rose to his feet. He just touched Tom's hand, refusing a proper handshake. He would bide his time and get even with Gil Archer at a later date. A similar thought was also going through Tom's mind. In the meantime he would keep an eye on Simmons.

When things had quietened down, Tom repeated his question that had provoked Simmons in the first place. 'You never answered my question.'

'What question?' asked Blake.

'Do you use this as your headquarters?'

'No, our leader has another place.'

'Shut up,' blurted out Simmons.

Tom would bide his time. The thieves had to get the spoils of their robbery to their master, and he would follow whoever had the task. He suspected that would be the place where James was being held.

Tom slept fitfully that night. He imagined that if

he slept deeply Simmons might take the opportunity to stick a knife into him. In the event, Simmons was the one who slept deeply.

They awoke to find an overcast wet morning. After they had eaten, Blake announced he had an errand to run. He would be delivering the spoils from the robbery, thought Tom. Now he wondered how to follow him without arousing suspicion in the others.

Charlie Blake saddled his horse and went back into the barn to collect two bulging panniers, which he strapped onto the horse.

Five minutes after he had gone, Tom wandered back into the barn.

'Is there a blacksmith in Moreton Bishop?'

Freddy answered. 'Yes. What's wrong?'

'My horse has a loose shoe. I must get it fixed. I can't risk a crippled animal.'

'It's just off the main street. You can't miss it.'

Tom walked his mount out of the wooded area, looking back over his shoulder from time to time. At the highway he mounted the horse and steadily trotted towards the town. Soon he pulled into a thicket of young trees just off the road. He looked and listened to make sure no one was following him. Nothing. He spurred his horse into a gallop. He knew that Blake wouldn't be travelling fast with the weight the animal was carrying.

Twenty minutes later Tom saw Blake far off in the distance. Blake's horse wasn't even trotting, he was just walking, seeming to enjoy the morning out. It had stopped raining and the morning was warm but still overcast.

Tom slowed his own horse to a walk so that he kept the same distance from Blake. They were now well past Moreton Bishop. Far ahead of him Blake

197

turned off the highway. He was now heading across rough moorland. Tom reined his steed to a standstill; there was no cover over the area. He decided that he had to let Blake move out of sight and risk losing him.

Minutes later he was moving off again, attempting to follow in the tracks of Blake's horse. The grassland dipped away and Tom reached round into his saddlebag to find his small telescope. He scanned the area. There was Blake heading towards a copse.

Minutes later Tom reached the area of trees. He thought he could just make out some buildings in the distance. He tied his horse up to a small tree and continued on foot, watching where he was treading, as he didn't want to have his feet cracking dead tree branches and warning someone of his approach.

As he got nearer he saw that the buildings consisted of a small cottage with two attached outbuildings. He stealthily approached the nearest outbuilding and crawled on hands and knees up to the outer wall. Some feet away was an old boarded window. As he moved towards it he could hear someone talking. He pressed his ear nearer.

'Right, let's have a look what you have in the sack.' Tinkling and rustling was all Tom could discern. He assumed that the sack was being emptied.

'Mm! Not too bad a haul. Where have you left the others?'

'At the old barn near Moreton Bishop. I told them that I would take their share back with me.'

'All right. I'll divide it up and you can take their share back with you. You haven't told them to expect any of the ransom money I'm expecting for this youth we have here, have you?'

Tom's ears pricked up at this.

'I haven't mentioned anything about him. They know about the kidnap because John Simmons had a part in it, and you know he can't keep his mouth shut. Only yesterday he started a fight with a new fellow we brought into our crew. The lad really knows how to handle himself, though. John didn't even hit him and he came off the worse. John finished nursing a sore fist last night.'

'What new man? Who said you could go around recruiting? What's his name?' To Tom's ears the mystery man sounded very disturbed at the news.

'Oh, don't worry, he seems a real rough-and-ready lad. His name's Gil Archer. We picked him up in Burton Saint Mary. He was doing some robbing for himself, and we gave him a trial. He almost killed a man at the house he robbed, right in front of my eyes.'

'Don't forget I want all of you here with me in the morning. We are collecting the ransom tomorrow, and if there is any trickery with Smyth I want enough men here with me to defeat him.'

Tom had heard enough. He now knew where James was being held. He carefully made his way back to his waiting horse, led it to the edge of the wood, mounted and galloped off towards the highway.

It was nightfall when he saw the familiar walls that formed the main entrance to his home, Credlington Manor.

He burst through the front door into the panelled entrance hall. He had forgotten how welcoming the atmosphere felt.

'Jonathan,' he shouted at the top of his voice. The study door flew open. Jonathan rushed out.

'Where on earth have you been?' He hugged Tom as though he hadn't seen him for years. 'Are you all right?'

Tom smiled. 'I know where James is being held. We need Silas and Caleb and to fully arm ourselves so we can rescue him.'

'Calm down, Tom. Tomorrow at first light will do.'

'But they may kill him at any time.'

'No, they won't. I promised to give them the ransom tomorrow morning. They would be really foolish to harm him now. I have agreed to leave the money in a particular place. In turn they will leave James tied to a tree about a hundred yards away but in sight of me. I am to give them time to escape and then collect James.' Tom sighed with relief at the plan.

'We shall get you a good meal and you can get yourself cleaned up. After a good night's sleep we'll set off very early and catch these devils before they set off on the final stage of their plan.'

Chapter 9

It was still dark when the small band of avengers clattered out of the courtyard of Credlington Manor.

Jonathan Smyth looked resplendent in a long brown riding coat, tricorn hat, black breeches and polished black riding boots. Beside him Tom was dressed similarly, except that his riding coat was his familiar dark green one. Silas and Caleb rode out together, with Dan, one of the most trusted of the estate staff, bringing up the rear of the party. Dan had served with the local yeomanry and was a keen fighting man when in the King's service. All five were armed with long-barrelled riding pistols, muskets and a sword each in a scabbard hung from their waist belts.

Out on the highway they urged their spirited horses into a canter. 'The sun will be up in about one hour. I hope that we will be on the far side of Burton Saint Mary by then,' called out Jonathan to his party.

The sun was beginning its rise above the skyline when they reached the outskirts of Burton Saint Mary. They quickly reached the main Exeter highway and Jonathan called a halt.

'We'll let the horses and riders have a break and study that plan you sketched last night, Tom. It would be very foolish for us just to ride in without planning our attack.'

Tom pulled out his rough drawing he had made

of the cottage and outbuildings he had crept upon the previous day. Jonathan studied the sketch.

'Caleb and Dan will approach the building from this side,' he pointed with his finger. 'Tom, Silas and myself will move in from the front. It is vitally important to be as silent as possible. Stealth and surprise will win the day.'

They remounted and headed north till they saw the signpost for Moreton Bishop, then headed west toward the little township. Not long after, Tom recognised the road he followed Blake on. Some five miles along the road he raised his arm to halt the little band. 'Here is the stretch of grassland with the wood in the distance.'

Jonathan studied the area. He reached into his saddlebag, produced his naval telescope and spent a long time scanning the scenery.

'Right, the plan of attack will have to be this. We carry on this road for possibly half a mile, then cut across through those trees in the distance. We then make our way along the tree line till we spy the cottage.' Tom looked disappointed. 'Look, lad, if we ride across this heath looking like a cavalry charge, we risk being spotted and they may decide to kill James.'

'Sorry, Jonathan.'

The riders made their way along the highway until they came to the cover of the trees. They then walked the horses through the wood until the rear of the cottage and outbuildings came into view. Jonathan halted the group.

'We should tether the horses here. It is still early, and my guess is that the other part of the gang has not arrived yet. Tom heard their leader telling his lieutenant that the whole gang had to be present here this morning. We'll wait here a while. One of us will go and scout round to try and find out if the rest of the outlaws have arrived.'

Tom tugged at Jonathan's coat. 'I'll go. I have seen the place before, and you haven't.'

'Be careful, Tom. We are so near to success. We can't ruin the show now,' whispered Jonathan.

Tom crept away from the others, watching where he was treading. A quarter of an hour later he returned.

'Have you been able to discover anything?' asked Jonathan.

'Everything appears quiet. If the others were here it would have been noisier.'

Out on the highway some four miles from their destination, four horsemen were making their way to the cottage.

'That street urchin you befriended never came back after taking his horse to the smithy,' sneered Simmons.

Charlie Blake had to admit that he was surprised and disappointed that Gil Archer hadn't returned yesterday, but he hadn't commented on the fact. 'He could have had a little thieving job of his own on, or he may have a lady friend that he doesn't want us to know about,' he responded.

'There can't be any lass that would take a shine to a scruff like him,' chortled Simmons. The rest of the group laughed out loud, all except Charlie Blake.

Simmons hadn't yet finished his complaints and barbs, meant to undermine Blake. 'Shall we finally see who our mystery leader is today then, Charlie? He appears good at sending out his orders but shy at showing himself,' Simmons sneered again.

'Whether you know him or not, you have done all right out of him. If I were you, I wouldn't ask too many questions. Just keep taking the spoils and keep your trap shut.'

Simmons scowled but decided not to make any further comment. The ride continued in silence.

Chapter 10

The morning sun was making its daily climb higher into the sky when Jonathan cast his telescope towards the distant road for the twentieth time. 'There are riders out on the road.'

'How many?' asked Tom.

'Four.'

'That will be them,' replied Tom.

Blake and his three comrades left the road and made their way across the heath. They didn't know it but two parties were tracking their movements: their leader also had a telescope pointed out of his window watching their progress.

He put the telescope back on the table, and reached for his long black cloak. As he opened the cottage door to exit he put on a black mask, which covered his eyes and most of his nose and cheeks. He pushed the nearest outbuilding door open and nodded to the guard keeping watch on James Purdy.

'Everything all right?'

'Aye. He's been fed.'

'Today is the day you are either set free or you die. If your master delivers the ransom, you are free. If he doesn't, you die,' said the cloaked man to James.

James didn't respond. He refused to converse with such creatures.

Minutes later the sound of horses being led up to the cottage was plainly heard by James. He didn't know it, but his rescuers also witnessed the same noise.

The two Blakes, Simmons and Alan Grey entered the outbuilding. All except for Charlie Blake stood and stared at the tall figure dressed in a long black cloak, black hat and a mask covering most of his face. They weren't sure what to say.

Freddy Blake broke the silence. 'Good morning to ye, sir.'

The cloaked figure responded, 'It's a lovely morning. I am glad to meet you all.'

'So what do you wish us to do?' asked Simmons.

'I trust you received your share of your recent foray? I also understand you have a new member. May I meet him?'

It was Simmons's chance to put one over on Charlie Blake. 'You could if he were here. He seems to have done a runner. We ain't seen him since he left yesterday.'

Blake butted in. 'He was a bit of a loner. I reckon he has some job on of his own and doesn't care to share the spoils.'

'You may well be better off without him. I am trying to form a feared and successful band of outlaws that will be rich beyond compare. One day you will all be famous and wealthy.'

'You haven't told us our task today,' reminded Simmons.

'Ah, yes. I have a lad in the corner who I have held for ransom. Today is the day his master intends to pay for his release. All you have to do is keep watch on the situation. If there is any retaliation from his master, I expect you to intervene. The future is looking very promising, Later I will tell you of profitable ventures I have planned. But now we must make ready for our journey.' With that the cloaked man dismissed any further questions.

Under the cover of the trees and undergrowth Jonathan, Tom, Silas, Caleb and Dan lay waiting for the appropriate time to make their move, when all the bandits were ensconced in the cottage's outbuildings.

'Caleb and Dan, you make your attack from the rear door of the building. Silas, Tom and myself will go in from the front door. Watch for my signal and then go in quickly. Surprise will win the day.'

Caleb and Dan crept quietly towards the rear doorway. Jonathan, Tom and Silas moved silently towards the front. The loud chattering coming from inside made certain that the band of rescuers were able to position themselves without being seen or heard.

Jonathan knelt down in his position at the corner of the outbuilding and looked down the side of the long wall. Caleb waved to indicate they were ready.

Jonathan nodded to his two that the attack was about to take place. Tom and Silas nodded that they were also ready. Jonathan raised his arm and let it fall.

They sprang to their feet and rushed towards the doors. Tom lunged at the crumbling timber door with his foot. A loud splintering of wood, and the door disintegrated under his impact. Caleb let Dan charge at the rear door with his shoulder. The rotting door gave way to Dan's powerful frame. Tom and Silas shrieked as they entered, to instil panic into the room. Caleb and Dan were now also in the rear of the long building.

The outlaws had been taken by complete surprise. The look of shock on their faces demonstrated this fact.

'It's that damnable Gil Archer. You were right, he did have a job of his own – attacking us,' yelled Simmons.

Swords appeared rapidly from the robbers' scabbards. Tom clashed swords with Freddy Blake, who was nearest to the doorway. Blake brought his heavy blade down towards Tom's shoulder. Tom parried it away. Blake took another sideways lunge at Tom, who sidestepped safely out of the oncoming blade. The momentum of the powerful thrust slightly over-balanced Blake and Tom didn't waste the opportunity. He brought his sword up and across and over Blake's exposed back. Bright red blood erupted from Blake's black coat. He screamed in pain. Tom was in an unforgiving and unmerciful mood. He plunged the blade into Blake's chest, killing him outright.

Tom took stock of the situation. Jonathan was battling with Charlie Blake, and Blake wasn't winning. Caleb was fighting with the guard who had been keeping watch over James, Silas was engaged in a sword fight with Simmons. Alan Grey appeared to be at the losing end of a fistfight with Dan.

Tom took the opportunity to free James. He dashed past the melee of men in combat and into the dark corner of the outbuilding.

A dark, cloaked figure was hurriedly escaping through the rear door.

'James, are you all right?'

James had a broad grin on his face. 'I knew you would rescue me, Tom.'

Tom took out his dagger and severed the bonds holding James.

'Look out behind you!' screeched James.

Tom spun round to see Simmons bearing down on him and instinctively raised his arm to shield his head. Simmons hit Tom a heavy blow on his left arm with a long-barrelled pistol. Tom had heard a pistol shot earlier. It must have been Simmons now his gun was empty, so he was using it like a club. Tom rapidly pulled his sword from his belt and faced Simmons. He glanced across the room and saw Silas lying on the ground. Simmons had obviously been the victor.

'I haven't got a sword, Archer,' sneered Simmons.

'There is one on the floor over there. I'll give you the chance you wouldn't give me. You owe me the chance to finish our previous skirmish.'

Simmons picked up the sword and brandished it at Tom.

'By the way, my real name is Tom Bascombe. My friend is the one you blackguards kidnapped. It was a grave mistake the day you fell foul of us.'

'I kept telling Charlie Blake that there was something about you I didn't like.'

'On guard!' cried Tom.

Simmons lunged. Tom deftly sidestepped the blade and brought his own sword down on his opponent's blade. Simmons pulled his blade away and decided to try an overhead chop at Tom. Tom counteracted by stopping the slice in mid-flight. He parried the blade away harmlessly and swiftly brought his blade downwards and plunged it into Simmons's chest.

Simmons looked shocked it had all happened so quickly. He dropped to his knees and rolled over. His blood was now spilling over the hay-covered floor.

Tom gave James the now redundant sword. 'If you are up to it, the boys may need a helping hand. I am going after that masked man.'

Tom quickly found his horse, leaped upon it and galloped off after the masked man, who he could see in the far distance heading off across the heath. Tom spurred his horse faster. He was now at least a mile away from the cottage and gaining on the cloaked man. The terrain was now merging into rocky scenery. Tom realised he had to be careful, the last thing he needed was a lame horse.

In the distance the man was now pausing. He then reined his horse sideways and began galloping at right angles to his original route.

What's he up to? thought Tom. He spurred his horse on in a diagonal direction to cut the man off. Tom caught the fleeing individual up, and as he was beginning to draw near him the man pulled a pistol from his belt and fired. Tom crouched low into the horse's neck. The shot flew wide over his head. The man threw the pistol towards Tom, but it fell well short.

As Tom drew level with the man, he pulled his sword from his scabbard. The cloaked man reacted likewise. Both men exchanged a few harmless blows. The man seemed to lose his footing in his stirrup and slipped sideways. He toppled off his horse and rolled to the ground. Tom reined his mount to a standstill and leaped from the animal's back. The man jumped to his feet, sword at the ready. Tom approached him cautiously, brandishing his blade horizontally. The man lunged. Tom parried the blade away and lunged towards the man's chest. The man jumped back to escape the oncoming blade. He lost his footing and stumbled. Suddenly he disappeared from view. Tom dashed to where he had fallen. He now realised why the man had altered his route. They were both on the edge of a sheer cliff edge about ten feet deep. It wasn't that it was a deep drop; the man was not able to persuade his horse to jump the sheer edge.

Tom looked down at the man, who was writhing in agony at the foot of the cliff.

'My leg is broken,' cried the man.

'I recognise that voice,' Tom mumbled to himself.

He looked in his saddlebag and found a short strap he always carried in case he broke a rein on his horse's bridle.

He climbed down the cliff edge towards where the disabled man was lying, rolled the man over on to his front and bound his wrists. The man was howling in agony as Tom moved him.

'Shut up. You fell, nobody pushed you.'

He turned the man back onto his side and pulled the mask off his face.

'You!' Tom gasped.

'Yes, Bascombe, it's me.'

Tom heard a voice above. 'Are you all right, Tom?' He looked up to see Jonathan calling down at him.

'Yes, look who I have here.'

Jonathan scrambled down the cliff edge.

'Good God, Daniel Petty. So when you got sacked as my bank manager you decided to turn your talents to kidnapping and highway robbery,' grimaced Jonathan.

'How did you find out where we were keeping Purdy? You owe me an explanation at least.'

'I owe you nothing, Petty, but as you will be hanging from the hangman's scaffold, Tom here can tell you. It may comfort you before you meet your maker.'

'I am Gil Archer. I joined your band of robbers so that one of your men would lead me to your hiding place. Charlie Blake did just that yesterday,' explained Tom.

Petty grimaced. 'I hate both of your guts. Damn you both to hell.'

Jonathan and Tom stood back and laughed out loud at the pitiful creature lying trussed up on the ground. All he had left was to swear obscenities at his opponents. Jonathan and Tom ignored his howling at the pain he was suffering at being manhandled back up the cliff face. They bundled him face down across the back of his own horse and set off back towards the cottage.

'Is Silas hurt?' asked Tom. 'He was on the floor when I left.'

'His pride mainly. He got a blow at the side of his head that felled him. He has a nasty cut to his temple, but it is bandaged and he should be all right in a day or two.'

Back at the cottage Tom looked at the outlaws that were still breathing. Dan and Caleb had bound up Charlie Blake, Alan Grey and James's keeper. Charlie Blake had a cut on his arm that someone had put a crude bandage on.

'Hello, Charlie,' said Tom.

'John Simmons was right about you, Gil. He said you were trouble.'

'The name is Tom Bascombe. Your big mistake was following Daniel Petty and kidnapping my friend. One way or another I was determined to defeat you.'

Tom walked over to James and hugged him. The two lads embraced with a fondness that only years of friendship can produce. They had always been as close as brothers.

Tom went over to Silas and patted him on his shoulder. 'Thank you, old friend.'

Epilogue

What was left of the outlaw band was now in jail awaiting trial. Credlington Manor seemed to have returned to its normal routine. James was again looking after the day-to-day running of the farm and livestock business, and Tom was more and more running the financial side of Jonathan's banking business.

Jonathan Smyth had decided that Tom's down-to-earth and slightly ruthless but compassionate way of dealing with the running of the bank in its everyday trade was much better than he could have achieved himself. He therefore decided that at dinner one evening he would make an announcement.

He had invited Silas and Caleb to sit and eat with them that evening instead of the normal routine of eating in the kitchen, as Silas and Caleb were not accustomed to dressing for dinner.

'Before we eat I would like to tell you of a decision I have made. Tom is now running the financial side of the family probably better than I ever did. James seems to be a natural farmer and takes on the task without interference from me. Mind you, farming was never my good point.' Silas and Caleb looked at each other and winked. 'Consequently, I now think I am beginning to get under their ambitious feet.' Tom was about to interrupt but Jonathan raised his hand, preventing Tom's protest. 'I am now getting to an age where I should be relaxing more, anyway. Therefore as from today, all the staff will take their daily directives from Tom about running the household or any financial aspect, and from James with anything relating to our farming activities. I, meanwhile, will take a back seat and be here for you if and when I am needed. Now, please raise your glasses to Tom and James.'

Silas and Caleb cheered. They seemed more delighted than anyone else.

'You two didn't know what you were a-getting into that day long ago when you agreed to repair our ship, did you?' said Silas.

'Silas, I think I knew from our very first meeting that you and I had respect for each other that would develop more as time passed,' responded Tom.

They got up from their chairs and exchanged a hug with each other.

'You know, I have also been thinking that you should be looking for a wife each,' said Jonathan.

Tom smiled and said, 'It's funny you should mention that. In the last week I have sent a letter to a young lady who lives in Exeter. I have informed her that I would like very much to visit her. I was intending to set off tomorrow.'

'Oh, and how did you meet this lady?' asked Jonathan.

'She was a passenger in the coach that I helped hold up. I took her to a farmhouse for safety.'

The other four chuckled at Tom and his little secret.

The following morning Tom prepared himself for the ride to Exeter. The stable lad brought Tom's grey stallion to the front of the house. The leather harness was gleaming. Tom opened the front door to discover the beautiful spring morning. He had his green long riding coat over a black velvet tunic and a white shirt with a lace collar. His riding boots had been polished to near perfection. As he walked down the three front steps, he donned his hat and smiled.

An upstairs window opened. Jonathan's head popped out. 'If she doesn't fall for you, she must be a fool.' He laughed and closed the window.

Tom reached Exeter by mid-afternoon.

He rapped on a small townhouse door. Eventually a tallish man answered.

'Good afternoon, sir, my name is Tom Bascombe. I am here to see Miss Berry.'

The man smiled. 'She is expecting you. I am her father.'

Anne was dressed in a beautiful white dress. Her hair was trailing to her shoulders. She looked beautiful.

Tom was introduced to her mother, who told them she would go and order tea and cakes.

Anne was overwhelmed at the sight of Tom. The last time she had seen him, he had been dressed like a tramp. 'My goodness, you don't look like the man who rescued me the day of the coach robbery.'

'I was working in disguise at that time.' They chuckled.

The pair spent the afternoon chatting and walking round the neighbourhood. As the early evening drew on, Tom bade farewell to Anne, who welcomed the suggestion that he visit her again.

Tom made frequent visits to Anne's house during the next six months.

It was early autumn when on his return from visiting Anne he bounced into the Manor and announced to Jonathan, 'Anne and I are getting married.'

Jonathan was overjoyed. 'I shall arrange a wedding feast here.'

On the wedding day everybody who knew Tom and James had been invited.

Jonathan proposed a toast to the couple, and finished off by saying, 'James, you have to catch him up. I need to organise another wedding feast while I still remember how it's done.'

Everyone in the great hall laughed.

Later that evening Jonathan was sitting by the great fireplace. The house was now peaceful. He smiled to himself. 'It is good to have another lady in charge of the house.'